This is a work of fiction. Names, characters, places and incidents are either the product of the author's imagination or are used fictitiously and any resemblance to actual persons living or dead, business establishments, events or locales is entirely coincidental.



For permission requests, email the publisher at

motownmysteries@gmail.com

Published by Motown Mysteries LLC.

@ 2026 Mark Love

Paperback ISBN: 979-8-9951939-0-6

E-Book ISBN: 979-8-9951939-1-3

Library of Congress Control Number: On File.

Edited by Nancy Light

Cover art by Halea Kasishke

# Fade Away

## By

## Mark Love

Fade Away

## DEDICATION

For Kim, Cameron, Travis, Kayo, Ichika and Yutaka.

The stars in my sky.

## ACKNOWLEDGEMENTS

Special thanks to Helene Love Snell, Mary Morehouse and Jerry Sorn who served as beta readers for this tale. Their ongoing support and assistance in my efforts is priceless.

Any mistakes in the story are mine.

# Chapter One

Ever wonder what Hell's waiting room looks like?

Walk into any VA hospital.

That's my perception.

Between the cloying odors of antiseptic, urine, geriatrics and stale air, it doesn't really matter which location you're in. Old farts from World War II, Korea and Vietnam can't wait to share their memories. A lot of heroes never made it home. But there are many who do. These are the people who, after finishing their duty, attempt to return to civilian life. Some can fit right in. Others struggle with their demons and memories.

Nowadays it's not uncommon to hear the suffering and struggles of the kids coming back from Iraq and Afghanistan, missing arms and legs from roadside attacks, Improvised Explosive Devices and suicide bombers. Add to that the thousands of people who suffer from one form of Post

Traumatic Stress Disorder or another. The struggles these brave men and women face every day make my problems insignificant.

I've always been a loner. My luck has been anything but good lately. I was a Ranger, one of the army's elite regiments. The army was my life. Combat was my mistress. Survival included a torn parachute, sniper fire, IEDs, booby traps and a rotten marriage. I had been shot, stabbed, fragged, concussed and beaten. Marched on missions until my feet were about to fall off. It's all part of the job.

But I might not survive this.

Discharge.

Despite the implosion the economy has taken, or maybe because of it, and the two wars the US fought for nearly twenty years or more, the Army suddenly has a surplus of old, worn veterans. It could have been a random selection. More than likely, I pissed some general off. No matter how you slice it, I'm done.

Employment possibilities aren't that good for anybody right now, but if you're Black, they're worse. Last week I screwed up and got drunk. Then I was mugged. My head got bashed in. Broke a couple of ribs. Stabbed in the gut for good measure.

That's how I ended up in the local hospital.  Transferring to the VA wasn't really an option, which was fine with me. Watching the box never appealed to me.  Same goes for video games. I got my fill of playing those during the downtime in the army.  The doctors encouraged me to move around a bit. Slow walks would help me regain my strength.

There were other benefits to getting out of my room. The hospital was staffed with a lot of good-looking nurses.  At the end of the hall was a lounge area that overlooked a small garden. That's where I was, just watching the medical staff come and go, when Gwen approached. She's a day shift nurse. Gwen's a curvaceous blonde with a sultry voice and handsome features.

"Time for your meds, Vince." Gwen handed me a tray with a Styrofoam cup of water and a paper cup with two capsules in it.

"When they gonna release me?" I eased the cup from her hand and tossed the pills back.

"What's the matter, baby?" she teased. "Don't like my company?"

"Rather have you all to myself."

"My husband won't go for that." She wiggled the wedding ring beneath my nose. Gwen winked as she flashed a smile.

I shrugged. "Nobody's perfect."

"Amen, brother." She started to leave then hesitated. "Almost forgot.

You got a visitor."

I straightened up in the upholstered chair. Nobody in this city knew me. It was just where my cash ran out. I'd been thinking about hitching a ride to the west coast. Saving money never was my strong suit. "Who's looking for me?"

Gwen fished a business card out of her blue cardigan and extended it. "Mousy looking guy. Said you didn't know him, but he'd like to talk, if you have the time."

I took the card and flipped it over. Herbert Bookman, Vice President of Reznik International. I'd never heard of it, or him.

"Want me to send him back?" Gwen sucked on her upper lip while studying me.

"Why not?"

I looked out at the gardens. Somebody put a lot of effort into tending the shrubs and flowers. It was nice but that was wasted on me. Having spent so many years in the swamps, deserts and jungles, I'd never been much of a nature lover. I turned my back to the view.

Timidly, he approached the lounge. I was the only one here. Other patients were probably in their rooms watching tv or undergoing tests.

"Mr. Tyrell? Mr. Vincent Tyrell?" The voice matched his appearance, dull and meek.

"That's right. What can I do for you, Mr. Bookman?"

He came all the way across the lounge to stand before me, a scrawny little guy in an ill-fitting brown wool suit. Black wing tips desperately in need of polishing covered his narrow feet.  What hair he had was the color and texture of straw. It was fading fast. He wore a pair of small circular John Lennon glasses. Nervous hands twisted his tie then fluttered across his coat. I was in no hurry. Eventually, he spoke again.

"I'm here to offer you an employment opportunity, Mr. Tyrell."

"What kind of job?"

"Corporate security."

That made me laugh out loud. My present condition wasn't exactly an advertisement for my abilities. "Someone stealing your milk money?"

He uttered a nervous chuckle and tugged at his sleeves. This guy never stood still.

"Actually, the position would be with the company. Eventually you could work for our CEO. He read about your unfortunate circumstances and thought you might be suitable candidate to join our team."

"Who's your boss?"

"Douglas Reznik." Bookman paused, as if he mentioned royalty.

"Surely you've heard of him."

I shrugged. "Can't say I have. What does he need with me?"

Bookman tried to stand taller. "Mr. Reznik is one of the country's leading billionaires. He has a diverse portfolio of business interests in real estate, construction, transportation, pharmaceuticals and engineering. Mr. Reznik is always looking to expand his operations. With training and tenure, you could become a member of an international team, dedicated to the protection of Mr. Reznik and his interests."

I rose, feigning sudden interest in the gardens. Bookman's reflection appeared in the glass. "That was some pitch. You practice it in the mirror?"

"I beg your pardon!" He took a step back, appalled at my response.

"Forget it.  There must be others who meet Mr. Reznik's needs. Local people, or experienced security personnel. Better qualified. Why me?"

He moved closer to the windows. "Perhaps. But Mr. Reznik requested I interview you personally. He feels any man who faithfully served his country for eighteen years---"

"Twenty-six years." It was a pleasure correcting him.

Bookman nodded apologetically. "Twenty-six years, should be properly rewarded."

"I get a full pension from Uncle Sam for my service. And all the free medical care I can use." I swept my arm around the room.

"You are scheduled to be discharged next week. Why don't you consider the offer? If you'd like to learn more, call me. I can arrange to have a car bring you in for a tour of the facilities and a formal interview."

I had been turning his business card over in my hand. It was thick, with a heavy coating and the company logo in the center. Expensive. "I'll give your proposal some thought."

"Then my business is complete. Good day, Mr. Tyrell." He extended his hand.

"Bookman." I shook it briefly, not at all surprised at the clammy touch of his skin.

* * *

Ten days later I was issued two tan cotton uniforms and my employee ID badge.  After six months of duty, I would be elevated in rank.  That might include more elaborate training and responsibilities.  Eventually I could be transferred to the elite security team that managed the safety of Reznik and the senior management. I was hired for an entry level position, working for an ugly grizzly bear named Duggan. Wayne Duggan was at least three inches taller than my own six-foot and probably fifty pounds heavier than my two fifteen. His hair was slightly longer than a brush cut, with a greasy sheen that looked as if he'd been dipped in vegetable oil.

Duggan's tiny dark eyes were set deep in the sockets, almost nonexistent in a moon-pie face. Most of his bulk was turning to fat. This transition was undoubtedly aided by the box of chocolate donuts dominating his desk.  He didn't offer to share.  That was how our work relationship would be. This guy would never win a congeniality contest.

"Welcome to North Carolina's version of hell, Boy." He put a little extra emphasis on the last word.

"Doesn't look that bad." I ignored the racial jab and sat across from him in the supervisor's office. It was the size of a closet.  One large window on the right-hand wall offered a view of the room next door. That room was five times larger. It was packed with monitors for all the security cameras and a crew of three. Racks of servers lined up across the back wall.

"You've never worked for me," Duggan said with a scowl. "Let's get a few things straight. You report anything strange directly to me. Keep a close eye on those pencil necks. Nobody goes into the restricted areas without proper authorization."

I nodded. Too bad there wasn't an outside window to distract me.

Anything would have been a better view than Duggan. "Want me to check their shorts too?"

He had no sense of humor. "Don't fuck with me. Just do as you're told and draw your pay. We'll get along."

I bit back a smart-ass comment, remembering the main reason I was here. Money. Despite the job description of a security guard, I would earn close to fifty thousand a year.  Better to make some cash and leave the government pension alone. I'm frugal. My needs never amounted to much. Even after the perpetual alimony payments, I could live well. And that was before any promotions through the ranks to the elite squad.

"Questions?" Duggan grunted.

"Nope."

"Then get to work. Patrol the complex. Check the badges against the scanner on anyone who's outside a laboratory. Secure the buildings."

"Got it."

As the newest recruit, I drew the graveyard shift. Working midnight never bothered me. Laboratories would be dull. There's nothing exciting about wandering around with a bunch of white mice and lab rats. I gathered my gear and left the office. Part of my equipment was an electronic notebook equipped with a bar code scanner. You slipped the identification badge into the scanner, and it automatically spewed out all the pertinent information on the video screen. Ain't technology amazing?

I assumed the laboratory would be quiet during the midnight shift. But the place was fully staffed. More than thirty people working away at computer terminals, microscopes and various equipment I couldn't identify. So much for assumptions.

After I checked all five levels of the building, I headed back to the security office. This job wasn't going to be very difficult. Duggan looked up as I entered.

"Something wrong, Boy?"

"Nope. Just finished my round. Thought I'd grab a cup of coffee."

Duggan bounded out of his chair and covered the distance between us quickly. For a bulky guy, he was light on his feet. He caught my right arm and pulled me to the wall. A detailed map loomed before my eyes.

"No fucking way! You couldn't cover the complex this fast." His breath was sour and warm against my face.

"Complex?"

"Yeah, dipshit. Complex. The whole fucking area is the laboratory. Not just this building."

"What the fuck! There must be ten buildings on this diagram."

"Eleven. Get back to work, Boy."

This operation was a hell of a lot bigger than I'd expected. I resumed making my rounds. On the patrol, I noticed four other guards doing the same thing. Reznik International took their security seriously.  The facility covered more than ten acres and was surrounded on two sides by dense woods.  Metal cyclone fencing ran twelve feet high around the perimeter with coiled loops of barbed wire across the top.  Heavy duty outdoor spotlights were positioned every fifty feet. The place was a certifiable fortress.  What I couldn't figure out was whether all the precautions were to prevent access to strangers, or to keep something in.

# Chapter Two

North Carolina was beginning to grow on me.  Reznik International's chemical plant was located north of Raleigh. The city was teeming with activity.  There were hundreds of corporations like Reznik taking advantage of the pleasant year-round weather to attract people to the Research Triangle. Most of the locals I met were friendly. I could sense this turning into a long-term residence. A casual, relaxed attitude infected people. June was just around the corner. Every day I heard comments about trips to the ocean, or to lakes up north. Visions of sandy beaches and swimming filled my head.

Through a notice on the electronic bulletin board at work, I'd found a furnished studio apartment nearby. Nothing spectacular, but for me, it was suitable.  A futon, stove, refrigerator and a flat screen television were included. Reznik International's employees got paid through direct deposit.

A local bank offered free checking accounts, complete with a debit card. I picked up a portable stereo with my first check and stashed a roll of cash in an old cereal box. I like the feel of money in my pocket.

Music has always played a big part in my life. Most of the soldiers I served with preferred blues, rock and jazz. I acquired similar tastes. Give me Bob Seger, Chuck Berry, The Stones, Lynyrd Skynyrd or Ray Charles any time.  Add some classic Motown hits for a change of pace. Life was good. Some mornings after work, while it was still cool, I went for a run to keep in shape. My wounds were healing nicely, so I didn't overdo it. I used one of the streaming services on my phone, to keep the music going.

Probably the best feature of the apartment was the pool.  On days when I didn't run, I'd push myself through fifty laps, trying not to empty the pool in the process. My afternoons passed lounging in the sun, checking out the occasional bathing beauties. Four flight attendants shared an apartment and two of them usually made regular appearances, working on their tans. No one approached me. I kept to myself. It was a two-mile walk to work. At some point, I'd buy a used car.

Three weeks later, I'd fallen into a routine. Work was tiring but not difficult, five nights a week. It was easy to become complacent.

I reported for duty that night, about ten minutes early. Entering the grounds, I saw Herbert Bookman and two men talking. Bookman ignored

me as I approached, deeply involved in the conversation. Their discussion

died as I got closer.

"Hello, Mr. Bookman."

"Oh. Tyrell." He tugged nervously at his coat and tried to position

himself between me and the other two men.

"Want to thank you for helping me get the job. It's better than

anything I could find on my own."

"Yes, yes, of course. Well, you'd better hurry along." Bookman

pumped my hand like a struggling politician and tried to steer me past the

others. Someone else had a different idea.

"Introduce me to your friend, Herbert." The voice was deep and full,

not one to be denied. Authoritative.

Bookman cleared his throat. "Vincent Tyrell, this is Douglas Reznik."

He stepped out from behind his flunky and grabbed my hand with a

firm grip. "You're the soldier who was nearly killed after his discharge.

How's the recovery?"

"Good as new. No permanent damage. Guess the guy with the knife

only nicked me."

I got a good look at my generous employer. He was a couple of inches shy of six feet. The guy had some locker room muscles. Brown hair going gray at the temples, green eyes that didn't quite look at you. But all that was secondary, something I could recall only much later. It was his face that had an immediate impact on my brain. Either Reznik had picked the living daylight out of a childhood case of chicken pox, or he had an extremely difficult time with acne. His mug was pitted with hundreds of tiny scars and divots. I've seen soldiers get half their features blown off by IEDs who looked better than he did. A row of tiny surgical scars ran along the hairline and ducked behind his left ear. Maybe it was an attempt at plastic surgery by a young Dr. Frankenstein. It was an effort not to look away.

"Like to thank you as well for the job."

"Nonsense, Tyrell. It's the least we could do for one of the country's fighting men. Getting acclimated to our environment?"

"Yes, sir. No problems."

Reznik smiled widely. It did nothing to improve his looks. "Excellent. Always glad to have another experienced fighter on our team."

Bookman poked his nose in. "Excuse me. . . Douglas, but we're . . . ah . . . going to be late."

"Have to run, Tyrell. Welcome aboard and all that jazz." Reznik slapped my arm and slipped away, returning to his conversation with the other man. I caught part of it before they ducked through a security door.

"Now then Dr. Sandoval, about this compound. . ."


* * *


It was after two in the morning when I checked the farthest laboratory

on the site. Unlike the other structures, this was a single-story concrete

building with only two entrances. Just a loading dock and a steel pedestrian

door. That's all. The big door was a metal curtain, secured by two padlocks

and a gate on the interior, which made access anything but easy. The

common door had a palm print scanner and a numeric keypad. There was

also a barcode reader. I checked the big door from outside. A semi-truck and

trailer were backed into the well. The foul weather curtains shrouded the rear

of the trailer. Standard procedure. There was no room to climb up from the

trailer to enter the building. I headed inside.

". . . and I'm telling you the temperature is unstable. We should shut

the whole system down until more tests are completed." A thirtyish Black

man in a lab coat stood just inside the door, shouting over the roar of

machinery. He was waving his arms excitedly to emphasize his case.

"There has never been a better time to complete the experiment,

Bailey." A stocky bald man stepped from behind a desk and approached us.

"You're wrong, Dr. Sandoval. We can't ignore the safety protocols. It's too risky. I want no part of this. It's dangerous!" Bailey stepped aside as I went to make my rounds.

This was the research and development building, a recent addition to the complex. Rarely was it in use this late. The three of us were the only people onsite. Large computer servers lined one wall, with various lights blinking and tape cartridges humming. In the center of the laboratory was a row of machines that vaguely resembled a centrifuge I'd seen in a high school physics class. These were squat little devices on iron stands, about three feet tall with a series of spokes or arms extending out from the center. A clip at the end of each arm held a test tube or vial. One of the machines was dormant, a thin wisp of smoke rising from a panel in the back. The other nine were whirling at various speeds, creating a racket.

"Hey man, get away from there!" Bailey yelled at me.

"It is perfectly safe." Sandoval turned in my direction. "There is no cause for concern. He is overreacting."

"It's dangerous!" Bailey repeated.

"Something wrong, Dr. Sandoval?" He was the man I'd seen earlier with Reznik and Bookman.

"Nonsense. Everything is fine. Really, Bailey, I must insist . . ." He turned back toward the Black man and the noisy machines drowned out the remainder of his comments.

After confirming the overhead door was secured, I circled past the machines again. Every building in the complex had heavy duty central air conditioning units on the rooftops. Computer servers tend to throw off a lot of heat. Especially if they're running around the clock.  The AC units are always functioning, even during the midnight hours when the outside temperatures are cooler.

Part of the duties of the security team include recording the room temperature for each lab checked.  Monitoring this could help to identify a small problem before it becomes a big one.

A panel of windows along the south wall was occasionally left open by the evening crew. One of the other guards caught hell from Duggan about that last week. There was no sense in giving that rat bastard a reason to nag me. While still a long way from being civil, he hadn't gone out of his way to acknowledge me one way or the other since my first night on the job. I preferred to keep it that way. A bank of lights on the machines was blinking rapidly. The unit in the middle was rocking back and forth on its stand.

"Hey, man! Get the fuck away from there!" Bailey was yelling at the top of his lungs. He saw the machine vibrating and pushed Dr. Sandoval to the floor. I watched dumbfounded as he dashed toward me. "Move! Get out of the---"

The explosion ripped the air out of my lungs and flung me across the room, splat against the concrete wall.

# Chapter Three

Lights flashed everywhere when I came to. I was on my back; legs twisted beneath me. Sandoval loomed above, shining a flashlight in my face. Everything was tinted red. Blood oozed down from my forehead into my eyes. Beyond him, I could see flames sliding across the ceiling.

"He alive?" Duggan growled in the background.

"He may be. Barely." Sandoval turned away and straightened up.

"What happened here?" Bookman stepped into my line of sight, not bothering to acknowledge me.

Sandoval raised his palms in an innocent gesture. "Dr. Bailey was trying an unauthorized experiment with a new chemical compound. THX 319. It is completely unstable." Sandoval pointed beyond my line of sight, no doubt at the raging fire. The lying sack of shit!

"What about Bailey?" Bookman asked.

"He is dead. One of the machines exploded. I tried to stop him. Unfortunately, I was too late."

A firefighter rushed up. "Gotta evacuate the building. Now!"

"Can't you put it out?" Bookman asked.

"We can't get ahead of the fire. It's too intense for our equipment." He was waving them to the door with both arms. "Get beyond the trucks."

"What about more fire hoses?" Duggan asked.

"Water alone is insufficient," Sandoval said.

"Most of the roof has burned away. We'll order in a chopper. Try to hit it from above."

"Let it burn itself out," Duggan said.

"You need a Class B foam to beat this type of fire," the firefighter said. "Spraying it from the chopper will help. But it will take a while. Unless you want the civilians from Raleigh to help?"

"No," Duggan snapped, "we handle our own problems."

"Thought so. We'll take a shot at it. Now get the fuck outta here!" The fireman grabbed Sandoval's arm and hauled him toward the door.

"What about him?" Bookman pointed toward me.

Duggan looked down. "He's good as dead anyway. You want witnesses to what happened here?"

# Fade Away

"Hell no."

"Leave him. C'mon. This whole fucking place is gonna explode."

I watched in horror as they ran through the door.  The fire closed in, melting the building around me.

Somehow, I had to pull myself away. My hands worked and my arms could support most of my weight. My legs felt like limp pasta. The door was only ten feet from where I'd been thrown. One hundred and twenty inches. I could crawl that in no time.

Which was exactly what I had: no time. The building was collapsing all around me. Ceiling beams and light fixtures kept crashing down. The fire crews pulled back, beyond the reach of the heat.

It took a minute to roll over and start crawling. Visions of jungle warfare kept snapping back into my brain. How many miles had I crawled through swamps, sand and sewage, elbows and knees propelling me along? If I had enough time, I could probably figure it out.  But if I didn't get my ass in gear, it wouldn't matter. I had to move. A lousy ten feet.

How hard could that be?

Distraction always worked well in the past. By focusing on something irrelevant, my body would take over the task at hand and get it done. Rock music was a favorite tool. I turned my brain to selecting the perfect tune for my predicament and my arms went to work. Something fast paced with a driving beat. Lots of strong guitar licks and drums. Long live rock. I started to crawl.

My legs dragged behind me like two useless sticks of wood. It was up to my arms to get it done. And damned fast. I reached for anything to help move me along. Grasping at the base of one of the few machines that remained upright, I pulled carefully, not wanting to topple it. If it fell and blocked my path, I'd never get around it. If it landed on my back, I'd be dead.

The machine wobbled but held. I inched forward. The heat was increasing. What the hell were these guys working with that could burn so fucking hot? The doorway got closer. Nine feet to go. My hands and arms did it all. Reaching, probing, pulling me along. Blood continued to seep into my eyes, clouding my vision.

Eight more feet.

Adrenalin roared through my veins. I wiped some of the clotting blood from my face. My sight improved slightly. I risked a glance at the back of the building. It looked like an Iraqi village after a drone strike had been called in.

Fire shot through the gaping hole in the roof. Dense smoke billowed up toward the rafters, obliterating everything three feet above the floor.

## Fade Away

Where the solemn row of machinery had stood was now a twisted pile of smoldering black iron. The computer servers were all fused together. Whatever data they stored went up in smoke. This was as close to Hell as I ever wanted to be. I focused forward and resumed my crawl.

Seven feet to go.

Beside me was the spot where the computer consoles had been. I sensed my time was up. Somewhere near the loading dock a large acetylene tank had been resting on a wheeled cart. The heat finally passed its safety point. I heard a muffled groan and glanced back in time to see the tank explode. It shredded like a grenade, sending most of the metal shrapnel rushing directly toward me.

My screams were drowned out by the roar of the fire. I covered my head with my arms and prepared to die.

* * *

If I'd been standing, it would have all been over. But the bulk of the tank missed me. The largest chunk, with the orange metal cap still intact, took off like a rocket. It flashed over my head and slammed into the wall, imploding concrete all around me. A mammoth hole appeared. It was big enough to drive a personnel carrier through. Unfortunately, I didn't have one

with me.  I kept crawling.

Six feet to go.

"I tell you someone's in there!"

"There's movement by the door!"

Loud voices kept drifting toward me. I might have been hallucinating.

But my brain refused to acknowledge them. Moving forward was the only

thing I could concentrate on.

"There!  By the control station!"

Somebody grabbed me. Gloved hands rolled me onto my back and

roughly ran over my body. Blood continued to pour over my eyes, making

sight impossible.

"He's alive!" The voice was muffled and distorted from inside a

firefighter's helmet. A curved Plexiglas shield concealed his face.

"Not for long!" Someone else said.

"Get him the fuck out of here!" another unseen voice yelled.

"Can you walk?"

I couldn't answer. Nothing was working right.

They hustled me outside, away from the remains of the laboratory. I

was carried out to a gurney and lashed down. A quick ride took me to the

Reznik infirmary, near the entrance to the facility. Even in the middle of the night, the place was staffed with doctors and nurses.

"Found him inside the lab that blew. Poor bastard's barely alive," one of the firemen said as they rolled me in.

"We'll take him from here. Put him in the first room on the right," a female voice said.

"This guy is badly burned. You equipped for that kind of trauma?" the fireman asked as they stopped beside an examination table.

"We are a fully functional unit. Anything we cannot do, he'll be rushed to the nearest Emergency Room. Go! I'll take it from here." The doctor pulled the curtain on the cubicle.

Strong hands probed me. but I was barely conscious. Only when they began to swab away some of the blood from my face did I realize the doctor was a woman. She was beautiful. A female nurse was assisting, passing her fresh bandages and sutures. The doctor was Black, with a narrow aquiline nose and short cropped hair. With each swipe of the sponge, she looked better. A dark angel of mercy.

"Can you hear me?" she asked.

Weakly I nodded.

"You've got some nasty wounds here, baby, but we'll do our best to patch you up."

I tried to answer but couldn't form the words.

"Don't try to talk. Rest." She gave the nurse instructions. An intravenous port was inserted and taped to the back of my left hand.

The doctor lightly rubbed a gloved fingertip across my forehead. "We've got you on some meds for pain and to prevent infection. Good thing we have access to employee medical files. Don't want you going into shock from an allergic reaction."

The medical staff had a quick discussion. My eyes would not stay open. It wasn't worth the effort. I was gone.

# Chapter Four

When I came to it was in a small room, one lonely hospital bed in the center of stark white walls.  A cluster of medical leads were stuck to my chest, the cords connecting to a flat screen monitor on the left-hand wall. The IV port remained in my hand.

The same doctor was perched on an upholstered chair next to the bed, reviewing something on an electronic tablet. Her eyes were coal black, with little flecks of gold in them.  She had a long, graceful neck and high cheekbones that accented her eyes. Her skin was smooth and clear, a milk chocolate color. What I could see of her figure made me think of an athlete. She wore aquamarine scrubs under her lab coat. Her legs were crossed at the knee.  She smiled briefly when I blinked at her.

"Welcome back. You've been out quite a while. How you feeling?"

I tried my voice. It croaked, but it was enough to get the words out.

"Like I got kissed by stampeding dinosaurs."

"About what you look like." She smiled again. "You've got a concussion and numerous lacerations on your head and back. X-rays were negative. No broken bones. You got lucky."

"Couldn't move my legs before."

She rose and placed a cool hand on mine. "That's likely from the shock or a pinched nerve. I gave you a muscle relaxer. By tomorrow, your legs should be fine. Get some rest."

"What's your name, Doc?" I managed to ask.

"Dona McWilliams. I'll be right here when you wake up."

I drifted out.

Arguing voices forced their way into my head. I opened my eyes just enough to see Dona standing in the doorway, blocking the entrance. Beyond her were two faces I didn't like the looks of.

Sandoval and Bookman.

"You do not understand, Nurse McWilliams, but I must question Tyrell regarding the explosion." Sandoval's voice had taken on a superior tone. "He could have observed something that will help prevent future accidents from occurring."

"It's _Doctor_ McWilliams. I don't care who you are or what you want.

The man is barely alive. He's sedated and drifting in and out of

consciousness. Whatever questions you may have can wait until he recovers.

Or at least until later in the day."

"You do not seem to comprehend the importance of this matter. . ."

Sandoval began.

"Perhaps you'd like to discuss this with Mr. Reznik," Bookman

interrupted. "I'm sure our Chief Executive Officer could persuade you of the

need for expediency."

Dona pressed a button beside the door and shook her head. "I don't

give a damn if you dig up Mary Queen of Scots and bring her down for high

tea. This man is to be left alone.  Disturbing him now could set back his

recovery. Nobody wants that!" She looked up as an orderly appeared at the

door behind the two men. He was bigger than Duggan. "Thomas, show these

gentlemen to the exit. Then I want you to guard this room. No one comes in

without my permission."

"Yes ma'am," Thomas said, filling the doorway with his bulk.

"You have not heard the last of this," Sandoval snapped as the orderly

reached for him. "Such insubordination is unwarranted."

"Mr. Reznik will not be pleased with your lack of cooperation, Dr.

McWilliams." Bookman stepped beyond Thomas's grasp and turned for the exit. "Not pleased at all."

"Don't break my heart, Bookman. Leave my clinic. Don't come back unless you need a rabies shot." She pushed the door shut and twisted the lock. Dona leaned against it for a minute and drew a deep breath.

"Man sounds like he needs an enema," I muttered from the bed.

She glanced up quickly and forced a laugh. "Which one?"

"Either. Both. When can I get out of here?"

The laughter died in her throat. "Could be a week. Maybe two. It will depend on how quickly your body responds to treatment. What's the rush? Got a date to go dancing?"

"Those guys left me for dead." I managed to sit up despite the way the room was spinning. "They caused it."

"I thought the fire was an accident." Dona moved away from the door and took my hand. I thought it was for comfort, but she was manipulating my arm around to check my pulse. Apparently, she wanted confirmation of whatever the monitor showed.

After witnessing her stand against authority, trusting her with the truth was an easy decision. "The explosion was. But Sandoval was conducting the experiment, not Bailey. He wouldn't shut it down. Bailey kept insisting it wasn't safe. He died trying to push me away when one of the machines blew. Must have caused a chain reaction with all the chemicals."

"They really left you to die?" Her voice was a whisper.

"I managed to drag myself near the entrance. Couple of firemen found me. They're not going to let me out of this place alive, Doc."

"They certainly are in a hurry to talk to you," Dona said thoughtfully.

"Talking ain't what they got in mind. I gotta get outta here." I tried to work my legs off the bed.

"You're not strong enough to even stand!" Her voice was firm.

"If I stay here, I'm dead. They'll smother me with a pillow. Pump an air bubble into the IV line. Something.  C'mon, Doc! Much as I enjoy the company, you can't babysit me around the clock. Sooner or later, they will finish me off."

"This is crazy!" Dona's eyes were getting wider. She wrapped an arm around my waist while I got my feet to the floor. She was taller than I'd estimated, around five nine or ten, and strong enough to keep me from falling on my face. "You're seriously hurt. There's no way you can travel."

"Can't stay. I'm not waiting around until they get back. Please, help me get out of here."

Something in my appeal must have convinced her. She leaned me against the bed and got a wheelchair from the corner I hadn't noticed before.

It took her less than a minute to disconnect the various medical leads from my chest and remove the IV port. Dona covered me with a blanket and opened the door. Thomas was still on guard duty. Those massive arms remained folded across his chest.

"What's going on, Dr. McWilliams?"

"I'm transferring this patient to Duke Regional Hospital. He's going to need multiple skin grafts once he's stabilized."

"Want me to bring the ambulance around?" Thomas was all smiles when it came to Dona McWilliams. I couldn't blame him a bit.

"Appreciate that. I'll drive him over. Could you stop at the nurse's station and bring his chart?"

"Sure thing. Meet you at the ER entrance." With that he was gone, big legs pumping smoothly away.

"No more hospitals. They'll know where to find me," I whispered.

"Leave that to me," she whispered back.

Thomas was at the ER entrance by the time we got there. They loaded me, wheelchair and all, into the van. It wasn't a true ambulance, just one of a fleet of Ford vans with the Reznik International logo on the side. There were brackets on the floor where they locked the wheelchair in place. Dona got behind the wheel and headed for the gate. As we passed the administration building, she made a squeaky gasp and nudged the gas pedal a little harder.

"What's wrong?"

"You were right. They weren't going to let me stop them. Sandoval and Bookman are headed back to the infirmary right now, with a big fat guy from security."

"Duggan."

"He's the one," she said, "and they don't look happy."

"Haul ass, Doc."

"My thoughts exactly."


***


Dona caught on in a hurry. It was never her intention to take me to any hospital. That was simply to steer Bookman and the others in the wrong direction. Instead, she drove the van into the seediest part of Raleigh and stopped beside a bar.  Ten minutes later, she came back with an old Chevy. Somehow, she got me inside the car and stowed the wheelchair in the trunk. We took off and headed east. Much later she told me someone else drove the van to one of the hospital parking lots and abandoned it there.

Dona kept going east until we hit water. She twisted and turned over a series of roads that had me completely baffled. Dona was silent,

concentrating on the drive. I studied her profile in the glow of the dashboard

lights. The fashion world was missing out. She reminded me of pictures in a

history book of the bust of Queen Nefertiti. I had no idea where we were

going. Highway signs eluded my vision. Eventually she parked under a

cluster of trees. Two hundred yards away I could see an old cabin, half

hidden in the early dawn mist. The house was built on pilings and extended

out over the water. A flight of rickety stairs led from the ground to a deck

surrounding the living quarters.

"Now for the fun part," Dona said, turning to face me for the first time

during our escape.

"What's that?"

"Getting you inside the house. I'll fetch the chair. You can ride most

of the way. But those steps will be a bitch."

I managed a shrug. "Nothing comes easy."

"Got that right. C'mon."

I was able to climb up the twelve stairs with Dona supporting most of

my weight. Once I was safely inside, she ran back down and dragged the

wheelchair upstairs. The house was dark and musty. I could make out some

furniture. The fabric on the back of a sofa was damp.

"My granny's place. Haven't been here in months," Dona explained. "I keep the utilities paid. Just in case I need to get away for a while."

"Safe enough for now. Appreciate your help, Doc."

"Forget it. I don't like the way Sandoval and Bookman were trying to intimidate me.  Throwing their weight around. There have been quite a few accidents at the lab lately. The company is quick to hush things up." Dona opened the windows. The breeze from the river or ocean stirred the curtains.

"Any other incidents as bad as this one?" I reached over my shoulder and tried to scratch my back.

"No. This one was the worst by far. Don't do that." She lightly slapped my hand away. "Your back is covered with lacerations. It's going to take time to heal properly."

I shrugged. "It itches."

Dona gave me a funny look. "Your back is coated with two layers of lidocaine cream. The skin should still be numb. Tingly maybe, but not itchy. Let me take a look."

She moved over to the couch and helped me into a prone position. My uniform had been destroyed during the explosion and my subsequent crawl toward safety. I was dressed in pajama bottoms and a hospital johnny, both in a pukey shade of green. Dona untied the back of my shirt and gently pulled it apart.

"Oh my God!"

"What's the matter?" I craned my head around, trying to get a look at my back. It was impossible.

"It's peeling," Dona whispered.

"Like sunburn?"

"Yeah. Only worse. I've never seen anything like it."


* * *


Dona ran to a nearby town for groceries and supplies. The house consisted of three rooms. A kitchen, a combination living-dining room, and one bedroom. There was a small bathroom with a claw foot tub and a dangling shower head. Linoleum that was probably new in the fifties ran throughout the house. The furnishings were old but comfortable, not the throwaways and hand-me-downs of the few weekend cottages I visited in the past. Each room was large and open. It had the minimalist approach, not cluttered by trinkets and mementos.

Dona insisted I stay behind and rest. I was going to recline on the sofa, but she steered me into the bedroom. The bed was a small patch of heaven. The mattress was thick enough to disappear into, beneath a slow-motion ceiling fan. Dona removed fresh sheets from a plastic storage container and efficiently made up the bed. Attempts at arguing were pointless. She eased me down on the mattress then slipped out of the house, locking the door behind her.

When she returned, I was sound asleep. I never heard her put the supplies away or when she took a hot shower. In the dark recesses of sleep, I began having nightmares about the fire. Chunks of ceiling beams crushed my legs. The acetylene tank dropped lower as it exploded, sending the cap through my chest before shattering the cement wall behind me. I must have groaned loudly, struggling to get away. Only the coolness of her hand on the back of my neck made me aware of her presence.

"It's okay. Everything's going to be okay." Her voice was soft in my ear, the breath warm and delicate.

I managed to open one eye. Her skin was dripping wet from the shower, her body scarcely covered by an old cotton tee shirt. Her hand stroked my head, carefully avoiding the lump in the back of my skull.

"Get some rest. We'll talk later."

Sleep reclaimed me.

It was late afternoon when I woke up. Dona was sitting by the window, looking out at the water. She was wearing a pair of powder blue

shorts and a bright yellow tank top. Her legs and feet were bare. I didn't

move, just stared at her for a moment. She could have been a dancer with

those legs. They were even better than I imagined. Somewhere nearby I

could hear gulls crying and the rhythmic splashes of the surf.

"Where are we, anyway?"

She jumped in surprise. "You're alive."

That shook me a little. "You think I died?"

Dona ignored it. "Swanquarter. It's near Pamlico Sound. Hungry?"

"Yeah."

"That's a good sign. Can you sit up?"

Slowly I managed to do so.

"Even better. Bacon and eggs?" She headed for the kitchen.

"Great. Anything but scrambled."

She hesitated for a moment. "Scrambled is the only kind I make."

"Then it will do." I rose from the bed and went into the bathroom. My

urine was tinted red. That didn't concern me much, considering how badly

my kidneys ached. I must have taken one hell of a beating during the

explosion. In the cracked mirror above the basin, I got my first good look at

myself since the accident. Bloodshot eyes stared back, taking in the details.

## Fade Away

There was a crooked gash in my forehead, closed with stitches. Part of the

hair above my right ear had either been burned or cut away, and more

stitches were visible. Near the crown on the left I felt a lump the size of a

golf ball. I tried to untie the hospital johnny, but it was sticking to my back.

"Brunch is ready," Dona called.

It was a slow, short walk to the kitchen. The old wooden chair was

sturdy. I sat carefully, leaning forward. She set a plate down and watched

me eat. Half of the first egg was gone before I realized they were fried, over

easy. There were six strips of warm bacon. She must have cooked it earlier

and heated it up for me.

"You lied."

She flashed a quick smile. "Testing you. How's the body?"

"Sore, but most of the parts seem to be working. Can I shower?"

She shook her head. "Finish your food, then I want to do a complete

examination. Get you out of those hospital things."

I motioned at her shirt. "Don't suppose you've got any extra clothes

here for me?"

"Daddy was about your size. He always left some things here. I'll look

around later."

When I was done, she helped me stand up. Dona undid the strings on the gown, but it wouldn't come off my back. She rummaged in the kitchen

drawers and came back with a pair of shears.

"No sudden moves." Playfully, Dona waved a forefinger back and

forth in warning.

"Never argue with a woman bearing scissors."

She stood before me and cut through the fabric, starting at the base

and bringing the shears to a halt an inch from my chin. I swallowed

uncomfortably. Dona set the tool on the table. The front flaps of the gown

hung loosely on my shoulders, but I still couldn't remove it. Dona furrowed

her brow and gingerly worked one arm free, then the other and peeled the

shirt slowly off my back. There was a wet, slurping sound as the skin finally

gave up its contact with fabric. Then Dona stepped behind me to examine

my injuries.

"This can't be happening!"

"What's the matter?" I twisted around to look at her.

She looked ill. Whatever food she'd consumed was threatening to race

back up. Dona drew in big gulps of air and moved to the open windows

overlooking the water.

"What is it, Dona?"

She found an old mirror on the bureau and passed it to me. I went into the bathroom and put my back to basin. Looking in the hand mirror, I could see my reflection in the glass above the sink. My back looked like I'd been whipped with a cat o'nine tails. Bright red welts crisscrossed every inch of skin. More than a dozen of these oozed a thick yellow puss.  I glanced at the remnants of the shirt, on the floor by the kitchen table. I could see bits of skin stuck to the fabric, along with tiny drops of fluid. I looked back in the mirror, stunned. Was that really me?

The most horrifying part was the color. Yesterday I was covered with obsidian skin. Someone once told me my complexion was so black it was almost blue. Today my back was peeling. Large, mottled chunks of dead flesh. But the layer underneath it was a different shade. It was lighter.

Dona stood in the doorway, watching me, still drawing in big gulps of air. When my eyes met hers, the reality finally hit home.

My breakfast came up.

# Chapter Five

We were sitting on the porch, overlooking the bay. Two days have passed since our predawn arrival. A pot of coffee was on the floor by her feet. We were both wearing shorts and baggy tee shirts. No other people were around. There was no radio or television in the cabin, so we had no way of knowing what was happening back in Raleigh. No news didn't bother me. But the lack of music would eventually get on my nerves.

Once the shock settled in, Dona persuaded me to lay on the bed while she peeled off the dead layer. By the time she was done, my back was almost clean. Now my legs were beginning to shed. The old skin came off in long, snake-like strips. We'd avoided any serious discussions about my condition. But I had questions that needed answering.

"What's happening to me?"

"I've never seen anything like it. The chemicals from the explosion must have saturated your clothes.  Then it penetrated your skin and caused

some type of imbalance or reaction." Dona squeezed my hand.

"Never believe it if I hadn't seen it with my own eyes. What happens

next?" I wanted whiskey in the worse way, but there was none to be had.

"I don't think you're done. Several things are happening, Vince. Not

only is your skin peeling, but your other injuries are healing at a phenomenal

rate. Somehow your body can repair itself at ten times the normal pace. Last

night your back was still showing signs of those welts. This afternoon,

they've already faded. Almost faded away."

Instinctively, my hand went to the lump on my head. Dona noticed

and nodded.

"Uh huh. That too. The swelling's practically gone."

"What about the stitches in my scalp?"

She shrugged. "Under routine circumstances, I'd leave those in a week

before removing them. But at the rate your body is mending, we should take

them out today."

Dona went inside and came back with tweezers a small pair of

scissors. She snipped the ends of the thread and gently tugged them free.

"How is it?"

"The wound is almost completely closed up. If I'd left them in another

hour, it would have been painful to remove."

"What the hell is going on?" I wondered aloud.

Dona moved away from me. There was a rough wooden railing that ran around the perimeter of the porch, weather-beaten and warped. She stood there and looked out over the water. After a moment I joined her. My body felt great, compared to the first night. No muscle aches, no pain. I was limber and healthy. I stood beside her and followed her gaze across the gently lapping water.

"Why is my color changing?" My voice was quiet.

She hesitated. "I don't know. Maybe the amount of melanin in your system suffered some kind of shock during the accident."

"Melanin?"

"It's the chemical normally present in the body that determines the skin color. The pigment. Before, you were very dark. Dark as anyone I've ever met. Or seen. Now, your skin tone is significantly lighter. Maybe after prolonged exposure to the sun, it will return to its previous shade." Her voice tripped over the words.

"Do you believe that?" I asked.

Dona shook her head. "I don't know what to believe."

I reached up and scratched my chest, trying to understand what she was suggesting. Dona turned and put her hand on top of mine.

"It itches there too, doesn't it?"

I nodded. "Hadn't really noticed it."

"Take your shirt off."

My back was no longer tacky. The tee shirt came off easily. I glanced down at my chest and saw the flesh bubbling there as well. Dona pinched a spot near my left shoulder with her fingernails and gently pulled it down toward my stomach. The skin rolled off easily. I stared down at the charcoal color that peeked through.

"It's all changing." I turned away from the railing and went inside. Dona followed me to the bedroom, but she hesitated in the doorway.

"Don't run. Not from me."

"I'm a freak. That fucking bastard Sandoval may be the only person who can help me. It was his chemical formula. He caused the explosion. But he left me to die in that inferno."

She came in and sat on the bed. "Sandoval will be intrigued once he can see what's happening to you. Maybe he knows some way of reversing the process. Or halting it."

"Not sure what to do now. But I'd better do it on my own."

"Don't you dare try to shut me out, Vince!"

I looked at her closely. There was something in her eyes. It wasn't fear or anxiety: it was kindness. She wanted to help me. God knows, I needed somebody's help.

"That's the first time you've called me anything other than Tyrell."

"It is your name, isn't it?"

"I prefer Vin."

She patted the bed beside her. "C'mere, Vin."

I sat beside her and was surprised when she put her arms around me. When I started to protest, Dona swiveled around into my lap and started kissing me. Passionately. We ended up in a tangle, sprawled across the bed.

"Seems to me, we both need to release all this tension," Dona said as she removed her clothes.

"You're the doctor," I managed to say.

"Don't forget it."

***

Later that evening, the rest of my old skin came off.  Even my face peeled. I was slowly growing accustomed to the new skin tone, so the final stages didn't shock me. Much. When the facial skin came off, some of my features changed too. A little scar tissue around the nose vanished, along with a mole beside my right eye. My chin was narrower, my cheeks flatter and not nearly as predominant. I hardly recognized myself in the mirror. Something occurred to me. A quick inventory confirmed my hunch.

There should have been a nasty looking scar on the inside of my right forearm from a knife fight years ago. Gone. The jagged bullet wounds in my left thigh, a souvenir from Iraq should have been visible too. Nothing. The marks from my recent stupidity in Raleigh that landed me in the local hospital had disappeared as well.

Even the crude zigzag scars from a back-country doctor's surgical repairs across my stomach had vanished.  My entire body was without blemish or stain.

Dona ran a hand over my skin. "Soft as a baby's behind."

"Gives a new meaning to being born again."

Her hands skittered their way down my spine. "Amen."

My sense of touch had been heightened during our lovemaking. I thought maybe it was her skin that was so tender, more supple than any woman I'd ever caressed before. But afterward when we were just holding each other, I ran my hand down the curve of her side. At one point, I raised my finger a fraction, so that it was no longer touching Dona. Yet I could still feel her silkiness. Still sense her warmth. The actual sex act felt fresh as well, something beyond the first experience with a new partner. But I didn't mention any of this. I didn't want to disrupt the tranquil moment and trigger a clinical analysis.

We were curled up in bed, making plans. We would return to the Reznick International facility and see what was going on. If the security people were searching for me, we would keep running. If they had forgotten about me, I might be able to sneak inside and find Dr. Sandoval. Chances are they had given me up for dead. The hardest part would be for Dona.

"Only been there three months. Fresh out of medical school, trying to find a spot where I could cultivate all those years of training. Bookman recruited me."

"Why?" I asked. "Don't take this the wrong way, but what's so special about you? Medically speaking of course."

She nipped at my ear then pulled back. "A couple of weeks before commencement, I saved a kid in a car accident. He was thrown free of the wreck but landed in a drainage culvert beside the road. It was on my way home from work. I pulled him out of the water and did CPR until the ambulance and paramedics arrived. He survived."

"You make the news?" I worked my hand around her waist and eased her on top of me. It had been a long time since I'd been intimate with a woman as exquisite as Dona. She awakened a hunger I'd forgotten.

She nodded. "Big feature on all the local channels. Even got a certificate from the mayor. A few days later, Herbert Bookman showed up at my door." Dona snuggled against me, her head on my chest. I could see the contrast between her skin and my new flesh tone. It wasn't as dramatic as it would have been a week ago.

"Make you a good offer?"

"Two hundred thousand to join their medical staff. Profit sharing and bonuses after the first year. How about you?"

"A victim of the economy." I summarized my recruitment into the ranks of Reznik International.

"Sounds like Bookman goes after people who are in the public's eye to bolster the corporate image," Dona said. "Like, 'we're such a great company to work for. Everyone here is a hero.' Or some bullshit like that."

"Makes you wonder what they're trying to hide."

"Must be something big. Why else would they try to keep the fire and the other accidents from the public?"

"Looks like we gotta find out. Hope you weren't planning on being vested in the pension plan." I ran a hand down her back. Dona's presence and proximity triggered reactions from my body.

"Something tells me severance pay isn't an option. Or the vacation time I earned. When are we going?" She ran a silky foot along my leg.

"In the morning. We'd better get some sleep."

"First things first," Dona said as I responded to her touch. "Then you can sleep. It's a long time until morning."


***


We got back to Raleigh late the next afternoon. I snuck into the apartment where I'd been living and recovered my money stash and some clothes. To avoid temptation, I never carried my debit card with me. So I grabbed that as well. If the card still worked, I'd only use it once. Reznik's crew might be able to track it. My last paycheck should be in the bank waiting for me. There were two bundles of bills in the heat vents and a third inside a box of cereal. I had over four grand in cash. Dona tried to make a withdrawal from her bank's automated teller machine, but the accounts were closed. Reznik must have used his influence to freeze her assets.

Over lunch in a cafeteria, we found out things were anything but calm at Reznik International. A local newscast brought us up to date. The explosion was being categorized as sabotage. Supposedly a group of industrial spies, led by me and supplied with inside information from Dona McWilliams, set the fire. Pictures from our company ID cards were included. My current face didn't look anything like my old one. I led Dona out to the Chevy. The radio was playing low, a soft rock ballad urging us to give them something to talk about. Talk about mood music.

"There goes our plan, Vin. Now what?"

"We'll start out with new IDs. Figure out how to get some answers. And who will be our first target."

Dona looked at me closely. "What do you mean, target?"

"Reznik, Bookman, Sandoval, or Duggan. Which one?"

"Target, as in kill?" she asked softly.

"No. We need information and help." I considered the best approach.

"I know where Bookman lives."

"Bookman it is. Ever thought about being a blonde?" I moved out onto the main road.

"You're the one with the changing skin. Why don't you be the blonde?" Dona giggled.

"You've got better legs. Let's go see Hack."

"Who?" Dona was busy watching traffic, making sure no one was paying us any undue attention.

"Wait and see."

I found the thrift store on the third try and managed to get a parking spot close to the rear entrance. Dona clung to my arm as we slipped inside and down the stairs to the basement. A chubby woman with a floral housecoat sat at the bottom of the steps, staring at a washing machine that was rumbling along.

"Hack around?" I asked.

She looked up at me and rolled her eyes. "Who sent you?"

"Walter."

She reached under the step. Her hand came out holding a remote-control unit for a garage door. She pressed the button and a section of wall slid away. She jerked her head in that direction. We went. Dona didn't speak until we were through the opening and the door closed behind us.

"Who's Walter?"

"Main character in the book, `The Secret Life of Walter Mitty'. Guy was always dreaming about being someone else."

"I didn't know James Thurber was required reading for commandos," Dona said with a smirk.

"Liked to read old books between missions."

We went down a narrow passage, lit only by a low wattage bulb near the end. As we approached, another section of wall slid away revealing a large room. Two white women and a tall Black man were inside, along with several tables of equipment, cameras, computers and a copy machine.

"Who you?" The man asked as he pushed off a stool near the door.

"Vance. This is Mona. We're looking for Hack."

"How you know about Hack?"

"Jimmy Reynolds. Served together in Iraq."

The Black man's face split into a grin. "Jimmy was a good boy. What can I do for you?"

I decided to go for broke. "We need fresh IDs for openers, some clothes and new hair for the lady, a piece, and maybe a car."

Hack snorted and rubbed a hand the size of a catcher's mitt across his face. "That all? How you fixed for rubbers?"

"Don't use them." I managed to keep a straight face.

"Brave bastard," he chuckled. "Let's get busy." He waved over the two women and the process began.

We gave them our birth dates. They checked the state records for death certificates issued for infants or children close to our own ages. Names weren't a problem. We didn't intend to keep these identities for long. Dona became Denise Kolas. I was now Terence Miller. Dona was taken into another room where her hair was tinted. She opted for red, instead of the proposed blonde. Hack studied my face for a minute. Without discussion, he ran an electric razor over my skull.

"Bald Black men are everywhere. You blend in this way."

I was in no position to argue. The hair would eventually grow back if I lived long enough.

Our pictures were taken for our new identities. Dona went to a rack of clothes and started to select a blue dress. One of the women gently placed a hand on her arm.

"You need something different, baby. People recognize you by the clothes you wear. Pick something out of character. Something for your wild side." She returned the dress to the rack.

Dona tried again. She picked out a short denim skirt and a bright pink cotton blouse. She went behind a curtain to change while I settled with Hack. He leaned across the table and rolled up a panel.

"I got Smith and Wesson, Glock, Beretta and Colt. Any preference?"

"You've got a Glock 17?" I was impressed. The lightweight polymer guns were almost magical. Even metal detectors had a difficult time spotting them.

"Seventeen rounds. Throw in a box of ammo to go with it and a spare clip." He held the gun before me, rolling one thick thumb down the barrel.

"How much?"

"Three hundred."

I hesitated. "What's wrong with it?"

"Nothing. Volume discount for all you gettin'. You want it or not?"

"Yeah, I'll take it. What about the ride?"

Hack shook his head as he handed over the gun. "See Spider upstairs. I don't mess with cars. Too much trouble."

"You're strictly underground," I checked the action on the piece and tucked it in my back pocket.

"Ain't seen the light of day in years. Like it that way."

He gave me a figure for the new identities. We had birth certificates, social security numbers and driver's licenses. Dona watched me dole out the cash and pay the man.

"Too bad you don't take credit cards," she mumbled.

Hack looked up and grinned. "Baby, I make credit cards. I sell you a couple, but they ain't worth the trouble."

"We'll pass." I hooked Dona's arm and led her back upstairs.

She looked like a call girl, with the red tinted hair and revealing outfit. Both the skirt and blouse were at least one size too small, which accented her figure but hardly looked comfortable. I didn't have to worry about anyone recognizing us now.

# Chapter Six

Dona checked out Bookman's apartment. He lived on the east side of Raleigh in a new building with a view of a large park. Bookman wasn't home and his car wasn't in the assigned space in the lot. We parked our new ride down the block and waited. Spider turned out to be a young Cuban guy who ran the thrift store above Hack's operation. He directed us to a used car lot, where we made a deal with the owner. The Chevy we had been driving and two hundred dollars, in exchange for a four-year-old Toyota with new license plates. I didn't want to be caught driving a stolen car by an ambitious cop hot for an arrest.

"How long do we wait?" Dona asked.

"Until he shows." I'd been curious about this and now seemed the appropriate time to ask. "How do you know where he lives?"

She looked at me steadily. "It's not like that. When he recruited me, Bookman brought me out to see the facility before I accepted the offer. On the way, we stopped for lunch. You know how he never sits still? He bumped the waitress and she spilled coffee on his lap. We came by here so he could change his clothes."

"Nice place?" The radio volume was low, but I could hear the ballad's theme of maintaining faith in one another.  It was appropriate. Maybe Bookman could help us get some answers.

"Don't know. I waited in the car." Dona calmly met my eyes.

"Then I guess we should go look and see."

We walked back to the apartment building. It was a high rise, maybe twenty stories tall. My new driver's license slid the interior lock back and we got past the lobby door. Dona checked the directory before and found Bookman's apartment. 1610. We went up.

"Ever make it with a redhead in an elevator?" Dona wiggled her eyebrows at me. She'd even dyed those red, to appear more natural.

"Nope. But I was hoping for a blonde."

She slapped my arm playfully. "Next time."

On the sixteenth floor, we wandered down to number ten. It was early evening, a time when most people would be coming home from work. Number ten was a corner unit, the farthest away from the elevator. The hallway was thickly carpeted. Ornate light fixtures were staged every thirty feet, throwing enough illumination to allow easy access into the rooms. Occasionally, a potted plant was positioned along the wall, beneath a graphic art poster.

Dona rapped Bookman's door. We tried to look innocent and inconspicuous. Not very easy. I bent down and studied the lock. There was no exterior bolt, just a standard door with a lock in the knob. It couldn't be too difficult to open.

"Got a bobby pin?" I muttered.

"You're kidding me, right?"

I glanced at Dona's cropped hair. Before the dye job, she'd buzzed it even closer on the sides. There wasn't any need for a bobby pin. Her hair wasn't long enough.

"Ideas?"

"Look around. Maybe he has a key hidden somewhere."

"Bookman struck me as the nervous type. Could be he's forgetful too." Dona wiggled down the hall. It was an alluring show I couldn't resist watching.  It's not like I could pry open the door with my bare hands.

"How about this?" Dona called.

She was kneeling beside a planter. A leafy green bush was arranged there, with a bed of cedar chips and rocks covering the potting soil. I went to join her.

"Think Bookman could lift this thing?" she asked.

"Doubtful. But let's check it out." I grasped the base of the planter and hoisted it in the air. Nothing was taped on the bottom of the container. As I set it down, some of the rocks shifted and tumbled onto the carpet.

"Isn't that cute?" Dona said. She held up one of the rocks for me to see. It was plastic, with a hollow slot covered by black electrical tape. She peeled it back and withdrew a key.

"Go try it."

Dona sashayed down the hall, no easy feat in that tight skirt and slid the key into the lock. The door opened silently. She removed the key and threw it back to me, keeping the door propped open with her foot. I returned it to the fake rock and joined her just as the elevator bell chimed.

Bookman knew how to live. The apartment included two spacious bedrooms. The kitchen and dining room were immediately off the door. Turn a corner and there was living room, with a clear view of the park. Each bedroom had its own bath. One was converted into a study, with a large wooden desk and computer system dominating the space. The bedroom had a queen bed. The room was bare. Bookman didn't strike me as someone who would do much entertaining in there.

We sat in the living room. There was still daylight. No lights were needed, but I wouldn't have turned them on anyway. I had no intention of alerting Bookman. The dining room and living room were nicely furnished, with a southwestern motif. Navajo rugs were draped over the two upholstered swivel chairs and the sofa, along with samples of antique pottery. Thick white carpet ran through the place. The wallpaper had sandstone and turquoise highlights. The overall effect was calming and serene, not overpowering. Quite a contrast to the stark plain décor in the bedroom and office.

I searched the apartment, looking for anything I could use against him. No weapons, no dirty magazines, nothing. Everything was squeaky clean. Bookman was the type of guy who probably called his mother at the same time every Sunday afternoon.

"What if he doesn't come home tonight?" Dona asked.

"Sooner or later, he's got to show up. With the lies they're telling the media, we're not free to roam the city. We're safer here."

"I'm getting hungry."

"Check the kitchen. Maybe Bookman's got the pantry stocked for guests. Just don't make a lot of noise."

She came back a few minutes later with salami and deli mustard on rye, dill pickles and beer. We ate quietly watching the door. When we were done, Dona stretched out on the couch to nap. I sat on the floor, right beside her head. To my right was the big window overlooking the park.

Waiting and listening.

***

An hour later, a key scratched in the lock. Dona sat up when I stroked her cheek. She was instantly awake. I stepped into the kitchen alcove, out of sight. Bookman entered and locked the door behind him. He walked right past me and into the living room, snapping lights on.

"Good evening, Herbert," Dona said. She rose to face him.

He jerked to a halt. "Who are you? How did you get in my place?"

"I charmed my way in." Hands on her hips, glaring at him.

"What do you want?" Bookman took an involuntary step backwards and bumped into me. He spun around fast. "Who the fuck are you?!"

"Don't remember us?" I pushed him across the room. He tumbled into one of the chairs.

"I don't know you! Either of you!" His eyes bounced back forth at us.

"Think back, Herbie. It hasn't been that long," Dona said. She bent at the waist and put her hands on the sides of the chair, bringing her face within inches of his. Recognition finally lit his eyes.

"Dr. McWilliams! You look so. . . different." Bookman relaxed just a little bit.

Dona glanced at me over her shoulder. "Not as dumb as he looks."

"Who's your friend?" Bookman started to rise out of his chair. Dona shoved him back.

"You remember Tyrell. He's the poor slob you and Duggan left for dead the other night. The one you're blaming for the explosion. And Bailey's death." Dona loomed over him.

"It can't be! You look so . . . different." Bookman managed to peer around Dona's arms. He was studying my face, trying to detect the mask or where the makeup ended.

"Let him up," I said.

Reluctantly Dona stepped aside.

Bookman came over for a closer look. He tentatively rubbed his fingers across my bare arm, then my cheek as well.

"My God," he whispered. "This is remarkable. It's real."

"Bet your ass I'm real. And I want my old face back. It wasn't all that great, but I kinda liked it."

"This is fantastic. . . All of this has happened within the last . . .ninety-six hours?" Bookman eyes were bright and jittery with excitement.

"That's right."

"Is all of your skin like this? I mean . . . all over?" He was trembling, his scrawny hands flitting around like a hummingbird.

"Yeah, all over."

"My God. We must go to the lab. Immediately." He started to move for the door. I pushed him back toward the sofa.

"Not so fast. Cops are looking for us everywhere. News and social media too. I want all the charges dropped. Now!"

He faltered. "I can't do that. Mr. Reznik made those arrangements. He has connections. We expected to find your body somewhere. What was left of it, that is. You look perfectly healthy." Bookman fluttered his hands at me. "This is fantastic."

"Yeah, so you've said. What are you going to do about the cops?" I wondered if we'd made a mistake coming here. Maybe Bookman was nothing more than an overpaid errand boy.

"I'll call Mr. Reznik immediately. He was due to fly to San Francisco for a meeting. I can catch him on the plane." Bookman reached in his pocket for the cell phone.

"Hold it!" I glanced at Dona. She raised her palms and shrugged. We had to trust him. Dona checked his coat pockets, then gave him the phone.

"Do it. But no tricks, Bookman."

"Absolutely not," he said. He hit a speed dial number. Bookman put the phone on speaker so we could all hear the conversation. Reznik's jet was already airborne. It took a few minutes for the call to be rerouted to the plane. The boss sounded annoyed when he answered.

"This better be important," Reznik snapped.

"It is sir.  I'm with Tyrell and Dr. McWilliams."

"Say again?"

Bookman cleared his throat. "At my apartment. Dr. McWilliams has been treating Tyrell.  His recovery is…amazing."

"I was under the impression his injuries were severe. Critical."

"That's an understatement," Dona said.

"Bring them to the facility. Immediately!" Reznik snapped.

I glared at Bookman. He cleared his throat again. "We need to notify the police that they are no longer suspects in the explosion."

Reznik must have covered his phone for a muffled conversation. A minute later he was back online.

"I've ordered the pilot to return to Raleigh. And the authorities are being informed of the change in status. Satisfied?"

Dona raised her eyebrows at me. I nodded. "That's a start."

"Then I will see you shortly," Reznik said. "ETA is ninety minutes."

With a click the call ended. Bookman tucked the phone back in his coat pocket.

"Mr. Reznik is anxious to see you both," he said.

"Didn't sound too anxious to me," I said. "Sounded annoyed."

"Douglas doesn't like surprises. He's very driven. Instead of flying to California for a meeting with potential investors, he's changed plans. He's coming to see you."

Before I could respond, there was a sudden thump in the outer hallway. I went to the door and checked the peephole. Nothing. The lock was still in place. From the living room Dona screamed.

"Vin! Help me!"

The Glock jumped into my hand as I turned around.

Bookman was behind Dona, his left arm around her waist. His right hand held a switchblade. It was pressed against her long, lovely neck. They were standing by the windows, overlooking the park. From a distance they probably looked like two lovers in a twisted embrace.

"Put the gun down, Tyrell," Bookman hissed.

"Fuck you, Herbie." I dropped to one knee. From this distance, he was an easy target. But could I get him in time?

"You're a jackass. Any calls to Reznik after hours trigger an alert to Duggan. He heard every word. Duggan wants your ass. He wants it real fucking bad." Bookman dug the sharp tip of the knife into Dona's skin, hard enough to draw a trickle of blood.

Dona's eyes were locked on mine. "Where'd he get the blade?"

"It was in his sleeve. I never considered him to be the type to carry a weapon." Her voice squeaked under the strain.

"Probably pulled the wings off of bugs when he was a kid," I said.

Harming Dona was the last thing I wanted. My right hand was locked in position. Sweat dripped in my eyes. I ignored it. He was hiding behind her, using her body as a shield.

"Shut up!" Bookman yelled. "Put the gun down, Boy. I'll kill her."

My body turned cold. "I hate being called Boy." It was now or never. My grip tightened on the trigger and the Glock roared.

Bookman must have been watching my fingers more than anything else. Even as I fired, he twisted the knife and slashed it across Dona's throat. My first shot deflected off his left cheek and stripped it bare. The second slammed into his left shoulder. The force drove him against the picture window, cracking it.

Bookman was still standing, blood oozing from his face. Dona remained pinned in his arm, her limp figure shielding him. Blood gushed down her body, pooling on the carpet at her feet.

"Life's a bitch, ain't it? A shame I had to kill her. But they wouldn't let you both live anyway." He panted as if he'd run up ten flights of stairs.

I rose from my knee, still holding the gun out before me. "You got it wrong, Bookman. No way I let _you_ live."

He thumped his chest with the heel of his left hand, a maniacal grin on his narrow face. "Body armor, Boy. Not a bullet made can penetrate it. You can't kill me." That said, he let Dona's body slump to the floor and began to laugh, softly at first, then louder.

"You'll never get out of the building. Duggan and his crew will be covering every exit. Who do you think knocked on my door? The cleaning lady? The paper boy? That was his signal. Everyone's in position."

I took a step closer. The gun rested firmly in my hands. If Bookman felt the blood oozing from his wounds, he didn't show it. Perhaps he was tougher than I'd anticipated.

"Take the plunge, Herbie." My whisper was barely audible above his annoying laughter.

He brought his arm back quickly, intending to throw the switch blade. I started firing before he got his elbow up. Two rounds went in his forehead. The rest of the bullets slammed into his chest.

The force of the impact dashed him against the windows. By the fourth shot, the glass began to shatter under the pressure. As the gun emptied, he was knocked out into the evening air, where he plummeted sixteen stories down. He was dead before going out the window. His swan dive to the asphalt would create a diversion enabling me to get away. If I got moving. Now.

But I stood in the living room, feeling the rage course through me. Dona lay crumpled on the floor, her blood permanently staining the thick white carpet.

During my years in the army, I'd seen my fair share of death. Iraqi suicide bombers once killed two soldiers who had been standing on either side of me. I hadn't been scratched. Sniper fire had taken more than one good fighting man from a position nearby. I'd killed enemies whose faces I never saw, punching holes in their uniforms with an automatic rifle because that was my job. I'd grown calloused about death. The Grim Reaper was just a cartoon figure who showed up a lot in horror movies and thriller magazines. People die every day. Some are innocent. Many aren't.

But this time my heart wasn't covered with a callous. This was different. Here was a woman I'd only known a few short days, who'd risked her life to help me. We had shared a lot: flight, rebellion against authority, laughter, even love. Dona deserved better than this. I felt a strange wetness in my eyes as I squatted there, desperately trying to find a pulse. Nothing. Bending low, I pressed my lips to hers, one final time.

"One down. . . Three to go, Dona. . .  I'll get them all."

# Chapter Seven

I slid the spare clip into the Glock, tucked the weapon in my back pocket and left the apartment. As I went out the door, I scooped a business newspaper from the stack by the sofa. Duggan would likely have guards posted on the stairwells, one flight below. I went up the stairs two floors. The elevator ride to the ground floor was uneventful. Duggan was one of four uniformed men in the lobby, anxiously waiting for the car doors to open. I walked right past them, absorbed in the lead story on the Wall Street Journal. Nobody recognized me. A small group of people gathered around Bookman's corpse. In the distance, sirens wailed.

Dona's purse was still in the car, along with my cash and clothes. I drove slowly away. There would be another time for me to take on Duggan, another place. One on one. But first, I needed to formulate a plan. I drove west to Burlington, wanting to put some distance between us. On the radio soulful songs about loss and heartache accompanied me. I refrained from singing along. Eventually I checked into a decent hotel, using my Terence Miller ID and paying cash.

I showered and sprawled on the bed, switching channels on the large flat screen television until it was time for the late edition of the local news. Bookman earned a minute and a half near the top of the hour. Police were tentatively calling it a murder suicide. Dona's body had not been identified.

As I watched, my back began to itch. Instinctively, I reached over my shoulder and dug my nails in. My hand came away with a layer of dead skin. I was peeling again. I wondered what I'd look like this time. Duggan wouldn't recognize me whenever we met. He's next.

***

I spent two days in the hotel undergoing another metamorphosis. If this kept up, I'd be lily white before Halloween. I could blend in with all the ghosts on the prowl.

And what would happen then?

Maybe I'd fit right in with other Black albinos.

If I lived that long.

The news accounts continued to run my employee picture from Reznik International and the twisted details of the explosion. It was no longer a top story. With no interest in social media, I wasn't sure if there was any attention being paid there. It would not have surprised me if a handful of conspiracy theorists were ranting about it on a podcast somewhere.

Had it only been last week when it happened? It felt more like a year to me. The cops were calling Bookman and Dona's death a double homicide. They hadn't positively identified Dona, which avoided any connection to Reznik International. Or to me. She deserved better than a Jane Doe funeral. I couldn't step forward without jeopardizing my own safety. At some point a DNA match or fingerprint analysis would be made.

I spent a lot of time in Burlington at the library. There was plenty of background information available on the internet on both Sandoval and

Douglas Reznik.  If I wanted any kind of advantage going after them, I needed to know every available detail, no matter how insignificant.

Reznik was in Who's Who, Fortune magazine and numerous articles, everything from business magazines to the local papers.  Most of the clippings described commendations for his support of different community programs. A few larger stories focused on the growth of the company.  The only photos of him were distant group shots. No close-up portraits. With that moon-cratered mug, who could blame him?  Reznik supposedly started out as a roughneck on an oil rig when he was only fifteen. Through a mixture of luck, determination and hard work, he soon owned a piece of the company. When the oil boom hit in the early seventies, Reznik's fortunes boomed as well.  He dabbled in real estate, chemicals, and transportation, elbowing his way into different industries every few years. This guy may not have the Midas touch, but he came damn close. By the time the oil business started to go soft in the eighties, he had already sold most of his shares for a multimillion-dollar profit.

Dr. Sandoval was officially Bartolo Manuel Sandoval.  He was born fifty-three years ago in Brazil. Sandoval studied chemistry at Miami University in Ohio. After college he taught at a small community college in New Jersey until three years ago, when he came to work for Reznik International.  He was listed as the director of development for Reznik's chemical division.

There was nothing I could find for Duggan. Not surprising. He was kept in the background, managing a security team. I hadn't expected to learn anything about him online without more personal information. There was no way I could access any military data.

Or could I?

From a convenience store, I bought a prepaid cell phone. Sitting in the park across the street, I tried my luck. The late afternoon sunshine felt warm on my face after the chill of the library's air conditioning. It took three calls to track Prosser down. He was stationed at a base in South Carolina.

"Vin! How's the ugliest rat bastard to ever wear a uniform?"

"Not bad, Pro. At least I could get a job in the real world."

He chuckled deeply. "Who wants one?"

"Got a point. What type of shit detail you pull now?"

"Quartermaster supply. Not the kind of duty they give medals for, but it beats waiting for someone to throw bullets at you."

Prosser covered the phone briefly and spoke to someone else. When he came back, the humor had left his voice. "This a safe line?"

"Sure."

"Word came down from up north you went sour. Some fucking terrorist activity bullshit."

Reznik's long arm even reached the military. "It's a crock of shit. That explosion damn near killed me."

"How can I help?"

"I need a favor. And it might not amount to anything."

I could picture him pressing the phone to his ear. Probably both boots propped on the edge of his supply desk. Pro was a career guy. He'd won the luck of the draw when it came to the discharge. Maybe being white had something to do with it. Or maybe not. Two more years he'd retire with a full pension. Rumor had it there was enough saved to start the charter fishing business he'd always been talking about. He was built like a middle-weight fighter, with a bright shock of red hair streaked with gray. I'd lost track of the number of times we'd saved each other's hides.

"Call it."

"See whatever details you can find about a guy named Wayne Duggan. Early forties. Acts like a Marine with a bad case of jock itch." I spelled the name for him and threw in a rough description.

"Duggan involved in your troubles?"

"Up to his scruffy eyebrows, Pro."

"You know he served?"

"Just guessing, but he's got the attitude. Whatever you can scrounge on him will help."

"On it."

Prosser didn't need convincing. Unauthorized probing into military records wasn't exactly in his line of work. But the man had contacts everywhere. If anyone could do it, Pro could. But that didn't mean someone else wouldn't be aware of his search. This called for extreme caution.

"How do I reach you, Vin?"

"You don't.  I'll call you in eight hours. If you're not in, I'll call back eight later."

"So, if someone trips to me, I can't tell them where you are."

"Still smarter than you look."

"Ain't saying much. Hang tough, Vin."

"Rock and roll, brother."

I gathered my notes on Reznik and Sandoval and headed back for the comfort of the hotel. A dip in the pool looked inviting, but my back was peeling rapidly. I opted for a hot shower and a fast-food meal.

**Mark Love**

* * *

There's a fine line between cautious and paranoia. Sometimes I think it's right behind me.  Rather than call from the hotel on my new phone, I walked down the road to a country western bar and punched up Prosser's number. After the call earlier, I'd taken the battery out of the phone. No sense making it too easy if someone tapped his line. Or possibly tracked me.

"Supply, this is Corporal Malcolm."

"Looking for Prosser," I said in my most official tone.

"Master Sergeant Prosser is off duty until 0700. May I assist you?"

"Only if you want to pay his poker debts, corporal. I'll call back."

"Very good, sir." The call ended without further comment. I tucked the phone back in my pocket after pulling the battery again. There was no way the call could have been traced so quickly. I was tempted to stick around for a beer and a little music, but there was no point in getting careless. I took a long walk, stretching the muscles and forcing oxygen into my lungs.  Eventually I hiked back to the hotel.

When checking in, I grabbed my bag from the Toyota, along with Dona's purse. With the local news on the screen, I went through its contents. I'd put it off long enough.

I was hoping to find some kind of address book or card with emergency contact info. After everything she'd done for me, pawing through Dona's personal items was difficult. I was invading her privacy and destroying her trust. Even worse was the memory of letting her down. She was a doctor and a beautiful young woman. I expected a lot of personal items to be in her purse. Many women carry cosmetics, vitamins, a brush, perhaps even some birth control pills, a diaphragm or condoms. But not Dona. There was a slim wallet with her driver's license, a bank card, thirty-seven dollars in cash, a library card and a ring of keys. A small calendar with a few upcoming appointments listed. Half a roll of breath mints. That was it.

After a career in the military, I am accustomed to waiting. But not like this. I did a series of calisthenics and tried to get interested in a television documentary. Nothing worked. I needed action.

It only took ten minutes to come up with a plan.

***

At three in the morning, I dressed in dark jeans, a sport shirt and an old pair of boots. I drove back to Raleigh. With directions from a Lithuanian convenience store clerk, I found the address on Dona's license. The apartment building was dark. A sweep for anyone watching the place came up empty. I slowly worked my way inside.

Dona's ring held nine keys. Two were automotive, one to a bank's lock box, another for mail. That left five. I had to try them all before her apartment door opened. I slipped inside, easing the door shut and waited. The refrigerator hummed. I could hear the steady tick of a clock. There was nothing else.

Checking her apartment took some time. In the darkness there wasn't much I could find, so I sprawled on her bed and waited for the sunrise. The pillows held the light, dusky scent of her cologne. It triggered memories of the hours we'd spent at Swanquarter and the closeness we'd briefly shared. I dozed off thinking about Dona.  It was my fault she was dead. No amount of struggling, mental or physical, would bring her back.

By six thirty there was plenty of sunlight filtering through the vertical blinds. I did a more thorough search.  There were no hidden microphones or transmitters. I wouldn't have put it past Duggan to bug her place while we were on the run.  Her address book was on a little table by the bed. There was no listing for anyone named McWilliams. Either Dona knew all the relatives' numbers by heart, or there was no surviving family. I collected a few supplies in a canvas gym bag and let myself out.

A guy wearing a T shirt and jeans carried a step ladder down the hall. He made a show of setting it up under the exit sign. I watched him as he moved. Pale blond hair worn a little long but recently styled.  He looked barely old enough to be out of school.  High school.  He had a baby face, devoid of wrinkles or worry lines.  Probably shaved once a month, whether he needed it or not. His hands were narrow and smooth, without any signs of callous or abrasions. There was a new leather toolbelt cinched above his hips. He climbed two steps up the ladder. A flicker of anxiety went through me, quelled by the comfort of the Glock in my back pocket. I glanced at his feet. The shoes!

Only fifteen feet separated us. Three quick strides and I had it covered. I dropped a shoulder and rammed into the ladder, memories of blocking sleds and football pads rushing back. The ladder tipped against the wall with a crash. Even as it went, the guy was digging his hand for a pouch on the toolbelt.

For my money, you can never say enough good things about adrenaline. Mine was pumping so fast, I could have carried a car up the steps of the Lincoln Memorial. My movements were a blur. I swept the ladder out of the way and was on top of him before he bounced on the floor.

"Who sent you?"

"You're crazy! What the hell's the matter with you?"

He was on his back, trying to crawl away. I shifted and placed a forearm across his windpipe. He stopped moving.

"Let's try this again. Who sent you?"

He squawked, trying to get the words out. His lips and cheeks were starting to turn beet red. I reached into the pouch on the toolbelt and felt the familiar grip of a gun. A quick tug brought it out for inspection.

"My, my, my. A 38 Smith and Wesson with a two-inch barrel. That's a very nice little accessory for a handyman. But I think it clashes with those fancy Italian shoes you're wearing."

His hands clawed at my arm, trying to get the pressure off his throat. I pulled back. He wiggled to a sitting position and rubbed his throat. He kept the left arm tight against his side, as if he'd banged his funny bone on the fall from the ladder.

"What's your name, kid?"

"Fuck you."

I squatted down on my haunches, just beyond his reach. "Heard of you. Always pictured you being a <u>lot</u> bigger. And tougher." I thumbed the hammer back on his gun and jammed the muzzle tightly against his crotch. "How about we try this again?"

He swallowed hard. His eyes grew wide in disbelief, feeling the pressure of the weapon jammed against his jewels. "Cartwright."

I kept the pistol pressed in place. "Better. What are you doing here,

Cartwright?"

"Watching the apartment. They sent me over at six. Nobody expected anything to happen. We've been keeping an eye on the place for more than a week now."

"Who sent you?" I repeated.

He gulped. Maybe I was being too hard on him. Cartwright was just a kid. He probably spent two years in ROTC and two more at some desk job in California before signing with Reznik.

"Duggan." Cartwright made an evil face as he said it.

"About what I figured. You call it in?"

He shook his head. "You don't fit the description of the guy we're looking for. I was just supposed to keep tabs on the place. See if anyone entered." Cartwright's color was bad. He was having trouble breathing.

"Where's Duggan?"

"At the plant. Everyone's on alert. They say it could be trouble for the entire division. Some executive got killed by a hooker."

"When's your relief scheduled?"

Cartwright's eyes rolled and his head slumped to the side. His body drooped against the wall. I waited. If this was a trick, it was a new one on me.  I checked his pulse. Nothing. Carefully, I ran a hand over his body. The ribs on the left side had broken. The ladder must have snapped them off and driven them into a lung. One might have pierced his heart. I didn't wait around to find out.

# Chapter Eight

After driving around downtown Raleigh, I found a big shopping mall on the northwest side of town. Over breakfast I considered my options. I could blow town and not look back, or continue my attempts at tracking down Duggan, Reznik and Sandoval. The idea of letting Dona die in vain while I scampered off to safety didn't appeal to my sense of justice. The doctor was my only chance at reversing the process. How many shades could a body go through? I had to find them. Outside the diner, I turned on the cell phone. As before, I blocked the caller ID. He answered with all the civility of a pit bull with bad teeth.

"Quartermaster Supply, this is Prosser."

"Wanna see if my order came in," I said calmly. There was no need to identify myself. Pro knew my voice.

"Purchase order number?"

Something was up. He couldn't talk freely. I needed a code that he would recognize, yet no one else could. "25-453319-A"

"One moment." Pro laid the phone on the table. I counted to ten before he was back. "Hasn't arrived yet. Delivery due after 1300. Try again after 1500."

"Roger that." I broke the connection. Walking back toward the parking lot, I hoped he understood the numbers. Pro knew I was in trouble in this part of North Carolina. He'd know there were only two area codes to try. The first two numbers were just the year, the rest was the cell phone's number, with A standing for 1. My palms were sweating profusely. It took him fifteen minutes to call back. I nearly smacked myself on the head with the phone when it rang.

"Vin?"

"Yeah, Pro. Thought you'd figure it out. What's up?"

"Trouble. I got the skinny on Duggan, but not without someone tipping to my inquiry."

"Aw fuck."

I could visualize him shrugging down the line. "Ain't the first time and it won't be the last. Ready?"

I uncapped my pen and turned to a fresh page of my notebook, behind the details on Reznik and Sandoval. "Go."

"Served eighteen months with the Marines. Dishonorable discharge after some involvement in a black-market scandal. Also got his drunk on and belted around two officers when they confronted him. Duggan did six months in county jail for aggravated assault charges too."

"Sounds like him."

"Born and raised in Raleigh. Permanent address follows." Pro rattled off the details with as much emotion as a weather forecaster.

"Anything else?"

"Listed ex-wife Molly as next of kin. That covers it."

I tucked the notebook into my pocket. "I owe you. Again."

"Forget it. Just don't get your pecker shot off. If you're gone, that makes me the ugliest soldier alive. I'd rather you carry that title."

**Fade Away**

"You're all heart, brother."

"Rock and roll, Vin. And watch your ass. You're on your own."

"Ain't that the truth?"

***

My cellphone didn't include a map application. It took three stops to find a store that sold a Raleigh city map. Technology is great, when it works. I wondered what would happen to the current generation if their smartphones were ever knocked out of service.  How would they find their way from point A to point B?

Spreading the map across the car's hood, I memorized the path to follow to Duggan's address. Earlier, I checked directory information. There were no listings for Sandoval, Reznik or Duggan.  I folded the map and headed for the location.

The address in question was in the seedier part of Raleigh, where the older, less cared for homes were.  Several houses had dented cars up on blocks in the driveways. Half naked children scampered in the scruffy grass, chasing a blue tick hound in circles.  Some of the houses were well kept, the yards free of weeds and debris.  I parked on the street and went over my story one more time.

A chubby woman came out of the house as I was walking up the drive. She moved slowly, as if she had to concentrate carefully on each step. Coarse black hair filled with snarls draped to her shoulders. Large dark sunglasses covered her face. The old shorts and tank top she wore looked at least one size too small. Her grip tightened on the purse as she became aware

80

of my presence.

"Mrs. Duggan?"

She froze in mid-stride. "Who's asking?"

"Terry Miller. I served with Wayne, long time ago. Told me to look him up if I ever came through Raleigh."

"Served where, jail?"

"Marines. We spent about a few months in the same platoon."

She pushed the glasses up her nose and clutched the purse to her chest. "I haven't seen him in over a year. Long as he sends the alimony, I keep the cops away."

"Know where he lives?"

"Nope. And I don't care to.  He works at some chemical place north of town. Wicksteed, or something. You can find him there, if need be."

"Thanks." She wasn't going to be any help at all. "I'll check it out."

"Tell him I'm still waiting for that new car. He promised me."

"I'll remind him."

"You do that."  She remained on the sidewalk, clutching her purse like it was the crown jewels as I drove away. So much for family ties that bind.

***

Surveillance was something I was always good at. Sitting and watching could be boring. I used the time as a mental exercise, formulating different scenarios to deal with Duggan, Sandoval and Reznik.  Cartwright's relief would have found him by now. Someone in the apartment building may have stumbled upon him.  Maybe they'd write him off as just being clumsy and falling off his ladder.

I wasn't counting on it.

Duggan's ex-wife had been as helpful as a teaspoon in a flood. I knew my only chance would be to penetrate the Reznik property under some pretext. A glimmer of an idea rolled around in my head, but I needed more equipment than I had with me. My only contact in Raleigh was Hack. He put me in touch with a guy who specialized in bugs and tracking devices. I picked up a high frequency monitor and two miniature transmitters with magnetic bases. The signal could be tracked up to three miles away.

I parked half a mile down from the entrance to Reznik International. With a decent pair of binoculars, I could easily see all the traffic that entered the property. Each commercial unit was noted in my book. I needed to get back inside and get up close and personal with the trio who were responsible for my predicament. But I wasn't going to walk in guns blazing like some demented John Wayne. There would be no cavalry charge to save my narrow ass. As Prosser had so eloquently stated, I was on my own.

At the end of the day, my list included more than a dozen trucking companies. I picked up a copy of the Raleigh News & Observer and returned to my hotel room in Burlington.

Sometimes it's all a matter of dumb luck. The third rig I'd spotted, a laundry company, needed drivers. One quick call was all it took to get an interview at nine in the morning. I went out for sushi and lost myself in an old spy movie.

***

Sunshine Laundry Service used large straight trucks to haul everything from hotel linens to hospital gowns for the metropolitan Raleigh area. The operation housed all the equipment necessary to clean and dry enough products to fill a football stadium.  The washers and dryers roared in the background, penetrating the double thickness of wall baffling in the dispatcher's office. An old white guy named Stuart looked over my employment application.

"You ever drive a truck, Miller?"

"Not commercially. Spent a lot of time in the service behind the wheel of all kinds of equipment."

Stuart worked a toothpick from one side of his mouth to the other, his eyes still on the form.  If he asked for references or my military records, I'd be history.  He dropped the papers on his desk and jerked his head toward the door. "Let's go."

"Go where?"

"Test drive. Never trust anyone with one of the rigs until I've seen them behind the wheel."

We went out to the backyard. Stuart pointed at a rig that was twenty years old if it was a day. It was an old Ford cab, with a twenty-foot compartmentalized box and an overhead rack for the sacks of dirty gear. Stuart scrambled up into the passenger seat and played tongue games with his toothpick while I walked around the truck.

"Come on, already. Let's roll," he grumbled.

I rested an elbow on the fender and shook my head. "Not until I finish checking it out."

"I ain't got all day, Miller."

# Fade Away

"Five minutes could save you a thousand bucks."  I unhooked the latches and opened the hood.  The engine block was cold. I checked the oil, antifreeze, hoses and belts. Then I started it up, checked the signals, lights and brakes. Stuart remained in the cab, drumming his fingers on the dash.

Now I was ready to go. "Engine's a quart low on oil and it needs changing. Right rear tire on the inside is bald."

"It's good enough for a test drive around the block, Miller.  Then we'll see how you do in reverse.  Back it into the dock at door three."

I did as he ordered, gently nudging the dock bumpers at the end. I set the brakes then turned to face him. "How did I do?"

Stuart spat the toothpick out the window. "First guy in two years to actually check out a rig before roaring off. I like that.  You start tomorrow. Six thirty."

"This truck?"

"Hell no. We've got good ones for the actual deliveries."

***

Two days behind the wheel taught me a lot about Raleigh. I'd given up the hotel in Burlington for a small boarding house a few miles from the Sunshine office. Since the drivers were given specific routes every day, I knew it could be months before I'd ever get sent to Reznik's facilities with a load of shop towels and lab coats. I had neither patience nor time. Sooner or later, Duggan's gang of thugs or the police would track me down. It was up to me to set the pace.  Arriving early every morning gave me the opportunity to sneak a peek at the other driver's paperwork.  Because of the size of

Reznik's operation, a daily delivery was scheduled. It always went out on the same truck, driven by a young Puerto Rican named Miguel.

Most of the drivers hung out at a rock and roll saloon around the corner from the garage.  Miguel was there on Thursday night, nursing a beer and looking sullen, sitting by himself at the end of the bar. Most of the drivers for Sunshine's Linen Service were white. Maybe Miguel was their token Hispanic American. Wondered if I was their token Black?  I bought a beer and took the stool beside him.

"What do you want, Miller?" Miguel made slow circles on the counter with his beer bottle.

"A little conversation to go with a cold one."

"I drink alone," Miguel said. "Won't be doing much of that tonight."

"Why not?"

"Tomorrow's payday. I'm tapped out.  Don't have enough money to get laid, let alone have a few beers."

Something inside me did a flip. The jukebox switched tunes from a current hit to an oldie. Miguel was going to make this easy.  "Hell, kid. I'll buy a round. Maybe even a shot or two."

"Why?" He eyed me suspiciously.

"Because I hate to drink alone. And you and I make up the entire affirmative action campaign at Sunshine."

Miguel sneered a grin. "You can't stand those white boys either?"

I shrugged. "Don't mind working with them. Sure as fuck don't want to drink with them."

"Ever been to Puerto Rico?"

"Went to San Juan a couple of times. It's been a while."

# Fade Away

He named a small saloon near the beach that was famous for its rellenos stuffed with shrimp. I asked if he ever heard the story about how the big picture window got destroyed.

"Hey man, everybody knows that. Couple of army yahoos took on half the goddamn navy.  More bodies in the air that day than on any flight with American Airlines."

"Cost me a week in the stockade and seven hundred dollars for my share of the damages."

Miguel's eyes grew large in admiration. "That was you?"

"Me and another grunt.  Couple of sailors kept playing grab ass with our waitress. My buddy had a crush on her that wouldn't die. He took offense."  A two-fingered wave to the bartender brough pair of fresh brews.

"Must have been something to see."

"It was a memorable night."

Miguel clinked his beer bottle against mine. "To Puerto Rico."

"And it's lovely ladies."

Within an hour Miguel was on his way to becoming completely drunk.  He downed half a dozen shots of rum in record time. Plenty of people wandered about, including several busty women who reminded Miguel of home. It was easy to distract him.  Each shot he downed was quickly replaced. Mine remained untouched.  By closing time, Miguel's constitution was the same as mercury. He was flowing in every direction. It was an effort to get him into the back of my car. Miguel kept singing lyrics about wanting somebody to love. It was the last song from the jukebox.

This was a good start, but I had no way of knowing how his system would react with the booze.  Some guys can get hammered every night, sleep for three hours and be raring to face another day. Others might not recover from a binge like Miguel consumed for a week and a half. I headed into the southern part of the city, away from the fancy night clubs and the swankier homes.

It took me twenty minutes to find the right one. The pickings were slim at three in the morning. She was sitting on a stool in a donut shop, nursing a cup of coffee with enough cream and sugar to make a milkshake. Her age was somewhere between twenty and fifty. Bleached blonde hair curled into a frizzy mop, frayed denim shorts and a ribbed tank top worn tight across the chest. I took the stool beside her and ordered a coffee.

"Up for a little fun, big fella?" She didn't put much enthusiasm into it.

I sipped coffee. "What ya got in mind?"

She patted her hair and hooked her thumbs behind the straps of the top, stretching the fabric out to give me a brief flash of cleavage. "You name it, I've probably done it. Round the world. Straight. Bondage. Whatever gets you off. Prices negotiable."

"You worried I might be a cop? Or a pervert?"

"I know every vice cop in town. And I can take care of myself."

I finished my coffee. "What's your name?"

"Roxie. You?"

"Terry. Why don't we go outside and talk a little more?"

She pushed away the coffee and slipped off the stool. "Sure."

I threw cash on the counter and guided her by the elbow out to the car. Miguel was still passed out in the back seat, snoring softly. Roxie peeked in the window at him then shook her head slowly.

"Threesies cost extra. Even I have standards."

"Just you and him."

She pouted her lower lip. "Don't like me?"

"Course. But I need someone to keep Miguel company.  He's been feeling low. Had a bit too much to drink, cause he's lonely."

"Where you goin' with this, Terry?"

Across the road was a small motel. Half the letters in the vacancy sign were lit, the rest missing or burnt out. I jerked my head in that direction. "It ain't the Ritz, but it will do."

"You spring for the room?"

"Here's the deal.  You get a hundred up front. Stick with Miguel until the sun goes down, I'll double it.  Make him happy, help him forget his troubles. I'll be back by dark."

"If I split?" Roxie didn't waste time on the formalities.

"Then you're out the second hundred.  I'm trusting you to stay with my friend. Show him a good time. And you can get some sleep and not be hassled." I held up two fifties from my dwindling cash supply.

"He must be some friend." Roxie reached for the money.

"We got a deal?"

"Yeah. Help me get him into the room, okay? I don't want anyone to think I've taken up rolling drunks."

# Chapter Nine

The scene at the garage was not a pretty one four hours later. Most of the trucks were rolling out on their runs. Miguel was nowhere to be found. I'd napped in the car, making sure Roxie didn't try to leave before sunrise. If Miguel woke up early, my plan would turn to shit.

Stuart was pacing the loading dock, slamming carts against the wall. As the newest hire, mine was the shortest run. I went about my business, checking out my truck but doing it in slow motion. Finally, Stuart appeared at my side.

"That damn wetback didn't show up. You'll have to take his route, Miller. Use his rig. All the clean laundry is loaded and sorted by delivery." He handed me the keys to another unit and a clipboard full of invoices. "Call me if you have any trouble."

"You got it."

It wasn't much of a plan, yet it quickly came together. Miguel's run took me into the domain of Reznik International. Hopefully nobody paid much attention when the lowly laundry man cometh.

I eased through the gates at Reznik International and let the rig come to a stop beside the security shack. The guard adjusted the baton and walkie talkie hanging from his belt as he moved up to the truck's running board, keeping a grip on the handle of his service revolver.

# Fade Away

"Where's the kid?"

"Never showed." I handed over my clipboard with the delivery invoice attached and tried to appear calm.  Earlier I rearranged the delivery sequence, making this the last stop of the day. "Dispatcher screwed around for an hour before giving me the run."

The guard shook his head. "Dispatchers can fuck up a wet dream. The lab rats are having fits, looking for their gear. Miguel's usually here long before two."

"Bitch at Miguel. I'm just trying to fill in. Most of these stops I've never been to before."

The guard passed the papers back to me. "Dumb shit probably got loaded on Captain Morgan's rum again. Or got caught up with a kinky broad. I'll have to listen to his stories next week. You know where you're going?"

"Invoice says building three, wherever that is."

"Keep to the right side of the drive, you can't miss it. Numbers are above the loading doors."

"Thanks." I put the truck in gear and rolled into the complex.

Time to move quickly. I couldn't count on the possibility of running into Duggan, Sandoval or Reznik and taking them hostage. The Glock was strapped to my left shin, offering a faint glimmer of reassurance as I entered enemy territory. But there weren't enough rounds made to shift the odds in my favor. Any attempted physical conflict here and I'd be snuffed out in a heartbeat. The idea was to spot my target and stick to the plan. Anything beyond that would be improvised.

Between buildings one and two was a reserved parking lane for the shooters, department heads and other assorted bigwigs. Each space was tagged with a name plate that hung on a chain by the building. The slot for Dr. Sandoval was empty.  I wasn't expecting one for Reznik. His chauffeured driven limousine would park wherever he wanted it to.  But there was an older Dodge pickup truck in the space reserved for Wayne Duggan.  I made a note of the number then rolled on to building three.

After exchanging fresh linens and lab coats for soiled ones, I turned the rig around and headed for the exit. Duggan's truck was still in the slot. Now or never. I took my foot off the gas pedal and let the laundry truck stall right behind his bumper. Setting the parking brake, I slid to the ground and moved toward the hood. I made a show of opening the bonnet and probing around the engine for a minute. Turning from the engine, I dropped to one knee and slipped my right hand under the bumper of the Dodge. The magnet held tight as I pressed the transmitter into place.

"Something wrong, Boy?"

I looked up from my kneeling position into the gruesome face of Wayne Duggan.

***

"Dropped my keys." I scrambled to my feet.

Duggan eyed me closely for a moment then jerked his head toward the laundry rig and its open hood. "You gonna get that heap out of here?"

"It's been making noises the last hour or so. Maybe a belt's slipping."

He ducked under the hood and tugged at each of the thick rubber belts. "Probably got a pulley worked itself loose. Will it run?"

"I think so."

**Fade Away**

Duggan moved around to the front and knocked the hood back in place. "Then get it the fuck out of here. This ain't Joe's Friendly Garage."

I bit my lip, holding back the anger. "Yes sir."

He watched me climb into the cab and start the truck. I nodded, trying to appear friendly and rolled on toward the security gate. In the mirror I could see his eyes following me. I kept the truck moving slowly. Duggan didn't recognize me. If he somehow made the connection, all hell was about to break loose. The guard at the shack merely lifted the barrier and waved me through. Sweat rolled off my forehead in thick rivers. I blotted my eyes with my forearm and headed back toward town.

After rounding a curve, I pulled the rig to the shoulder and removed the monitor from the canvas bag that held my jacket and a few assorted tools. The signal was beeping steadily, but it wasn't moving. With luck Duggan would stay put until I dropped the truck at Sunshine.

I could use a little good luck for a change.

***

Sooner or later, Duggan had to leave the property. It was Friday night. No one could expect him to live at the facility, especially since there had been no sign of trouble from that evil terrorist Vincent Tyrell. They were probably hoping I'd made a run for the border. After leaving Sunshine's, I swung by the motel. The drapes were partially opened. Roxie was curled against Miguel on the narrow bed. She stirred when I knocked and came to the door naked, shielding her eyes against the late afternoon glare.

"You're early." She slammed the door behind me to block the sun.

Roxie made no attempt to cover up.  I caught a glimpse of stretch marks across her abdomen before averting my eyes. There was a tattoo of some type of flower on her hip. "How's Miguel?"

"The guy's an animal. He rose from the dead just before noon and we've been screwing ever since. Then he passed out a few minutes ago."

I peeled off another hundred bucks and passed it over. "We're even."

She folded the bills carefully and tucked them inside her shoe. Roxie blushed when she turned around. "Do I have to leave?"

"You want to stay?"

Roxie shrugged. "He is kind of cute. Thinks we met at some bar last night. You care?"

I grinned. "You're on your own. Whatever goes from here is between the two of you. Never saw you before."

"Thanks, Terry."

"Forget it."

I jumped back into the Toyota and headed for the Reznik property. There was still a chance to catch Duggan before he left.  I parked off the road half a mile away and settled down to wait.

An hour went by, then two. It was almost nine. I debated about giving up for the night when the transmitter beeped in a different pitch. It was moving toward the main gate.  I looked through the binoculars toward the entrance. The Dodge truck was headed this way.

"Showtime," I muttered, twisting the ignition key and giving the Toyota a chance to warm up.

There was just enough light left in the sky for me to see Duggan's ugly mug as he roared past my hiding spot. I gave him a ten count then pulled onto the road. There was no need to get close enough for him to spot me. Duggan held the truck at sixty-five, a good ten miles an hour over the limit. Obviously, he wasn't your typical law-abiding citizen. We went south then east across the top section of the city. The little transmitter continued to guide me in the right direction if I drifted too far back to keep him in sight.

Duggan stopped at a party store for a case of beer and some cheap cigars: probably his idea of a gourmet meal. I stayed in a parking lot across the street. The binoculars propped on the dash kept him in focus. Duggan never looked my way as he lurched back on the highway and continued east.

Ten minutes later, he pulled off the road into a new housing development. Airy colonials and Cape Cods filled the little courts that blossomed off the main drag, a variation on the square block neighborhoods of the fifties. Duggan rolled the truck to the last court on the right and swung into a driveway at the very bottom of the circle. I killed the lights and parked on the main road. Time for a closer look.

****

There were seven houses on the court. The two on each side of the street closest to the intersection were in various stages of being completed. The remaining three were finished, even down to the sod that had been rolled out. One overhead streetlight threw a wide spot in the middle of the cul-de-sac. Lights were blazing in the homes bordering Duggan's. Yelps of children playing came from the one on the right. That just might be a blessing. The noise could help conceal my approach.

I walked along the street casually. No one noticed.

Duggan's house needed a woman's touch. Any woman. There were no flowers in the little dirt garden beside the driveway. Instead of drapes, vertical blinds covered the windows. None of the cozy features that helped make a house a home was visible.  Wayne didn't want to dent his macho image. I eased along the side of the house, near the screened door that opened onto the driveway. Duggan's gruff voice boomed through the mesh.

"Papa Joe's? Yeah, I want a large with everything.  Extra pepperoni and anchovies. Yeah, that's the address. Twenty minutes or I get three bucks off.  Out."

I heard the familiar snap and hiss of a beer can being opened. The television came to life with a baseball game. Thank God for ESPN. Keeping low, I headed back to the car. I removed the Glock from my leg and racked the slide, jacking a fresh shell into the chamber. The spare clip was deep in my back pocket, but it wasn't something I was counting on.  If I went in there shooting, the whole neighborhood would be on alert. Not to mention the local cops. Silence was the best plan. I wanted to get up close and personal with Duggan to see what I could learn about the other two players. Unknowingly, he'd given me a way in.

Fifteen minutes passed before the delivery driver showed up. The car was a Chevy Camaro that probably hadn't seen new oil in a decade. I flagged the kid down before he could turn onto the court.

"That the large with extra pepperoni and anchovies?"

The kid behind the wheel nodded, eyeing me suspiciously for a moment. He couldn't have been more than a hundred pounds dripping wet, and most of this was hair that dangled in his eyes.

"I'm just out for a walk. Let me take it here." I extended a folded fifty toward him.

"I dunno," he said slowly, eyes on the money.

"Keep the change."

A cobra couldn't move as fast as the kid did.  He jammed the square box through the window and ground the gears trying to get the Chevy into reverse. I remained beside my car, watching the thick trail of blue exhaust until he turned on the highway. It was time for my entrance to the Duggan abode.  I drove the Toyota around the corner and parked in the driveway behind his truck. The old Tar Heels cap from Miguel's rig was now angled with the brim down low over my eyes.  The Glock was in my palm, under the warm pizza box.  I banged on the screen door and waited for Mr. Personality to come fetch his supper.

"You're late," Duggan grumbled as he reached the door. "I get three bucks off."

"Made a wrong turn."

"Ain't that a shame? Still gonna cost you."

I shrugged, still holding the pizza on the porch. "Can I use your phone to call it in? Mine's dead. The boss has to approve it."

Duggan kicked the door open. "Make it fast. Wanna watch the Yankees game in peace."

I moved past him and set the pizza on a counter that divided the kitchen from the living area. The place was a mess. Empty beer cans were scattered everywhere, along with takeout cartons from half a dozen fast food restaurants. Duggan probably believed cooking and cleaning were a waste of time. It was a surprise that he had a landline telephone. Probably required with his security position. I pretended to dial a number on the wall phone while he turned his attention back to the baseball game. The Glock was pressed against my thigh, waiting for the opportunity to use it.  Duggan tore open the pizza carton and folded two slices over, sandwich style and began devouring it.

His back was to me. Only ten feet separated us. If I moved quickly, I could knock him out and tie him up with a minimum of noise. Then we could play twenty questions.  I hung up the phone and started toward him, bringing the Glock up over my head like a club.

Duggan chose that moment to turn around for a fresh can of beer.  His eyes bulged and he spat out a chunk of pizza big enough to choke on.

"The fuck's going on?"

"Payback time, asshole."

Duggan shrugged his shoulders. "Fuck it. Keep the money, Boy. Ain't that big a deal."

I took a step closer, bringing the gun level with his sternum. With my free hand I pulled off the Tar Heels cap and flipped it toward him. That cocky gesture nearly cost me my life. He moved with the same quickness I'd seen on my first night at Reznik International, something his weight and slovenly manner had temporarily erased from my mind. His right foot lashed out and caught my wrist, knocking the automatic from my hand.  I was showboating and he damn near took me right there.

"Who the fuck are you?" He was crouching now, hands by his waist, shifting his balance and lowering his center of gravity.

My right hand was tingling. I mimicked his movements, circling to my left. We traded a series of jabs, each one just missing the target.  Duggan bounced a shot off my left ear, giving everything a ringing quality for the next few minutes.

"You forgot me already? Hasn't been that long since you left my ass for dead in the fire."

"Tyrell!" He kept moving, his eyes searching for a suitable weapon.

"In the flesh, you ugly fucking bastard." The Glock had landed back in the kitchen somewhere. With luck it had slid under the mountain of beer cans where he couldn't reach it any faster than me.

"That's some makeup job you got."

"Ain't no makeup, Duggan. It's the real thing."

He stopped circling and scrunched his eyes up for a better look. "Guess Bookman wasn't crazy when he called."

"Nope. Not going to do you much good."

"Pitching him out the window was slick." Beads of sweat were flowing off Duggan's brow, leaving little rivers down his cheeks into the open collar of his shirt.

"It was him or me. Bookman didn't give me a choice. All I wanted was a chance to get back to normal. Maybe Sandoval has the formula from the experiments when the lab blew."

He sneered with delight and stepped closer. "Nothing came out of that building except Sandoval.  And you. What's your game, Boy?"

"Payback time." I kept moving slowly, waiting for the move.

"Bookman thought he was hot shit with that blade. You can't take me, Boy.  I'm a Marine."

A grin crossed my lips. "Ex-marine."

"No such thing!"

He threw a quick left at my chin. I ducked under it and hooked a couple of fast shots to his ribs before sliding back. Duggan wobbled but kept his feet.

"Where's Sandoval?"

"Fuck you!"

"Not very original."

He tried another kick, like Jake Bates going for a fifty yarder. It was headed for my crotch. I sidestepped just in time, catching his ankle with both hands and yanked as hard as I could, pushing the foot up over my head. Duggan went down, banging his head on the floor. He managed to twist away and climb back to his feet.

"Gotta do better than that, Boy." Duggan was wheezing, struggling to find his breath. If I kept up the pace, he couldn't last much longer. He was big but out of shape. Duggan tried for an uppercut. I blocked it with my forearm and nailed him in the nose. I connected two hard jabs to the solar plexus. It was enough to drive him back into the wall. Duggan slid down to the floor, clutching his bleeding beak with both hands.

"You were never good enough. Not for the Marines. Not for me. Probably couldn't even make it in the Girl Scouts."

He pulled away his hands and stared at the blood smearing his fingers. "I eat Army shit like you for breakfast."

"Dinner time, asshole!" I spun with a wheel kick and caught him in the jaw, snapping his head against the wall. He collapsed on the floor, face down. Out for the count.

I puffed out a breath and waited for my heart rate to slow down to normal. "Still the champ."

# Chapter Ten

He was out for half an hour.  I secured his wrists and ankles with duct tape, then rolled him onto his stomach and tied him up like a calf at a rodeo. There wasn't any rope lying about. I used a plastic extension cord. Not exactly by the book, but it was functional as hell.  A search of his place turned up three handguns and an old hunting rifle that hadn't been cleaned since Teddy Roosevelt and the Rough Riders roared up San Juan Hill.

Inside the toilet tank was a plastic wrapped brick of cash, over five thousand dollars.  I put the money and the weapons in the trunk of the Toyota. The Glock was resting comfortably on my hip once again. The baseball game looked dull, so I switched it off.  Mounted on the wall beside the stove was an old radio. Two stations playing country music came in strong, but I opted for a weaker one cranking out classic rock. Perched on a stool and nibbling at his pizza, the music calmed me. It was difficult to ignore the urge me to take the money and run. I plucked the anchovies off another piece and watched my hostage. Drank one of his beers. Duggan finally came around with a groan.

"Ever wonder why pizza is round, sliced into triangles and delivered in a square box?"

He mumbled something to the floor.

"Welcome back, ex-marine."

Duggan tried unsuccessfully to roll over. "Fuck off!"

"You're a poor loser." I washed down the last bit of pizza with a sip of his beer. "All I want is the rundown on Sandoval and Reznik. Give me the information and I'm gone."

"The only way Reznik sees you is on the coroner's table." He slithered across the floor, still trying to work himself free. His face was covered in sweat, the skin waxy and gray. A nudge from my boot flipped him onto his side. Duggan looked ready to take a bite out of my leg.

"Quit talking out your ass. Look at me. I'm a freaking medical wonder. If Sandoval can take a sample of my skin, or blood, or whatever the hell it is he needs, maybe he can analyze it and find out why it's continuing to change."

Duggan's breathing became more labored. "Who the fuck cares?"

"A scientist like Sandoval. And old lizard face Reznik might enjoy having skin like this. It heals overnight from wounds that used to take a week to mend. Sounds like something a butt-ugly rat bastard like him would kill for. Be a hell of an improvement for Reznik."

Duggan stopped struggling for a moment. Maybe he was visualizing his employer without his moon cratered face, free of his side-show appearance. "Cut me loose. I'll call him."

I casually sipped the beer. "Fell for that gag once. Cost me a good friend. Where are they?"

He hesitated. I began to consider other forms of persuasion. On the counter was a knife block set filled with fancy blades. I took a paring knife from the block and gave it a little flick in his direction. It banged off the floor and clipped his cheek. A drop of bright red blood appeared. I selected another, slightly longer blade and threw that as well.  It stuck in the fading linoleum beside his nose. Duggan's little piggy eyes were darting rapidly from the knife to me. His mouth started to work then stopped. I doubted he had much loyalty. Maybe he was stubborn.

Then I drew the biggest blade out of the rack, a gleaming French knife, nearly a foot long and razor sharp.  I turned it over slowly, admiring the edge. It would slice his hide easily. Wayne Duggan started talking before I could get off the stool.

"Sandoval's going to a conference in Denver. He's supposed to be there for the next two weeks."

"Denver's a big town. Where?"

His greasy head drooped to the linoleum floor. "How the fuck do I know? I ain't his fucking secretary."

"What kind of conference?"

"Skin doctors.  You know the drill. Specialists with new material, maybe a few plastic surgeons thrown in for laughs."

"Sounds right up Sandoval's alley.  What about Reznik?" I finished the beer and set it on the counter beside the pizza carton.

Duggan didn't answer. If he was faking, he was doing a good job of it. I waited a minute then squatted down in front of him. He wasn't breathing. I jammed two fingers against the flabby skin of his throat, trying to find the carotid artery. Too many pizzas and beers had finally caught up with Wayne's ticker. Probably thought he was too mean to die.

I untied him and removed the duct tape from his wrists and ankles. The knives went back into the block. Everything I could remember touching was wiped down with wet paper towels from the kitchen. That included the phone, the counters, even the remote for the television set and the controls on the radio. I pressed Duggan's hand to the phone and the remote control. Switched the game back on. If the cops did treat this as a crime scene, there must be fingerprints. The pizza box, paper towels and the beer can all went with me. I closed the front door to his house. Sooner or later, someone would find him. But I needed time to get to Colorado.

Two down, Dona.

Two to go.

***

The flight from Raleigh to Denver's International Airport took a little over three hours. During the ride, I went over the details of my escape, looking for anything that the cops could use to track me down.

I'd removed the transmitter from Duggan's bumper and packed it along with the receiver. It might come in handy out west. I had no contacts like Hack in Colorado. The Glock was disassembled and buried in my checked bag. The weapons from Duggan's place were tossed in a river not far from the house. Bullets went down a sewer. The guns were taken apart. I didn't like the idea of some kid finding a loaded weapon.

I switched plates with a car parked at a crowded bar in Knightdale. The next day I sold the Toyota at a lot in Durham where they didn't ask questions. For a thousand bucks, Hack sent Spider to meet me at the Raleigh Durham Airport on Sunday with a new identity. Terence Miller vanished. I became Reggie Dunbar from Milwaukee.

The plane went into a slow bank over Nebraska as I eased my seat back a little. The blue haired granny sitting next to me had the Raleigh paper spread out over her tray, seriously attacking the crossword puzzle with a magnifying glass and a pencil.

"What's an eight-letter word for life ending? Ends in E?"

"Homicide."

She counted it out on her fingers then nodded her thanks. I closed my eyes and tried to work on different scenarios for locating Sandoval.

"How about a five lettered word for intentional combustion?"

I opened one eye. Granny was impatiently staring at me, gnarled fingers clutching her pencil. "Well?"

"Got any letters?"

"Second one is R."

"Arson."

She turned and scratched it in place, her fingers shaking as she wrote. I leaned closer and studied the puzzle. The title was Mayhem. The way things were going, that could be my new middle name.

***

A brown ring of smog obscured the view as we came into Denver. Colorado always stirs images in my head of pristine snow-covered slopes and Coors beer.  But the summertime haze blocked out the distant mountains.  You must drive for miles before you get a good look at anything larger than an anthill.  My new identification allowed me to rent a car from the Budget people, who reluctantly supplied me with a city map that looked like it came off a restaurant's placemat.

I found a moderately priced hotel on the north side of town. Using the free computer in the business section, I went through the Denver Post website for any mention of the skin conference. Better than half the coverage was devoted to the Rockies baseball franchise and the upcoming Broncos football season. Absolutely nothing about the current conventions in town.

The Yellow Pages didn't narrow down my search in the least. Better than fifty large hotels, any of which could have been holding a conference in one of their ballrooms. That didn't include the various private organizations which could be hosting the function. There had to be a way.

I felt restless from the long plane flight. The adrenaline from my battle with Duggan faded hours ago. The hotel's facilities included an exercise room and pool. Maybe a workout would trigger ideas.

I checked my reflection in the glass while slipping into a pair of shorts and a tee shirt. My current appearance no longer startled me. The skin tone was still a couple of shades lighter than my original color. It was almost graphite. Not quite milk chocolate now, but maybe after the next layer peeled away. This could begin soon, if I continued to shed on schedule.

The fitness center was a converted meeting room. Old pea green carpet worn through in spots supported the few pieces of equipment. An elliptical machine, stationary bike, incline bench, barbell set and a rack of smaller free weights was the extent of it. I rode the bike first then went through all the weights, piling them to the limit. I did as many reps as I could, letting my mind wander. An hour later I was breathing hard and dripping with sweat.

"Training for a marathon?"

I turned to see a young brunette striding steadily away on the elliptical machine.  She wore what looked like a purple tank top and white gym shorts.  Her skin gleamed with sweat. She must have been there for a while.

"Working out the kinks," I said, wiping my face with one of the hotel's thin towels.

"Must have been some pretty mean kinks." Her eyes met mine briefly.

"It's been a while. You have any idea where the pool is?"

She slowed the machine to a crawl, then stepped off the pedals and stretched. "End of the hall to the left. Do you swim as well as you throw those weights around?"

"Haven't sunk yet."

She took a couple of towels from the counter and headed for the door. "I could use a dip myself. Maybe even a race."

The top of her head barely came level with my shoulders. I fell into step beside her, shortening my stride to match hers as we headed down the hall. "Didn't say I was fast, just buoyant."

A smile tugged at the corners of her mouth, but it quickly faded away. "Big guy like you ought to be able to swim faster than little bitty me."

"Got the feeling you're setting me up."

We reached the pool and she peeled off her shorts. The tank top was actually a Speedo suit, cut high on the hip. It clung nicely to her figure, which was small but muscular. A guy couldn't help noticing how firm her ass was. I pulled off the tee shirt and checked out the pool.  It was rectangular, probably no deeper than six feet in the end.  No diving board or lifeguard.  We were the only ones there.

"Race you to the end.  Loser buys?"

I took a better look at her. She was a couple of inches over five feet tall, with light gray eyes. Her nose had been broken once and never properly reset. Maybe the result of a childhood fall that she'd grown accustomed to. It gave her face character. She was a white girl with the start of a good tan the color of cinnamon, enhanced by the darker brown hair that brushed the tops of her shoulders. Her hands and feet were tiny but proportionate to her overall size.

"Buys what?" I asked.

She shrugged those tan shoulders slightly. "That's up to you: drinks, ice cream, and maybe dinner."

"Let's start with drinks." I stepped forward and curled my toes around the lip of the pool.

"Great."

She dove into the water and took off like an eel. I followed, although there was little chance of catching her. She moved with an easy grace, gliding through the water with smooth, steady strokes. I did more thrashing and churning, making a big production of my effort not to drown. She was clinging to the edge at the deep end a good twenty seconds before I arrived.

"Looks like you lose."

I splashed her playfully. "You're a damn mermaid. I should get a head start."

She splashed back. "What do you want? Half the pool?"

"Twenty seconds, double or nothing."

"Un nuh.  Fifteen, for dinner. "

"You're a cocky little mermaid."

She smiled and splashed me again.  I liked the way the smile wrinkled the corners of her mouth. There was mischief dancing in her eyes. "Yes or no, cowboy?"

"Why not?" I kicked off the side of the pool and began to stroke steadily toward the other end. She passed me with less than five feet to go and was already climbing out when I got to the ladder.

"I've suddenly developed a craving for lobster and filet mignon. Or maybe sushi, that really sounds good. Denver should also have some great Mexican restaurants." She picked up one of the towels and began briskly drying her hair.

"Hope you know a good restaurant. I'm new in town."

She gave me that shy smile again and stuck out a hand. "Michelle Atwater. Everyone calls me Mickie."

"Reggie Dunbar." Her hand disappeared completely in my grip.

"Give me some time to get cleaned up and we'll head for dinner. How's half an hour sound?"

"That works. Meet you in the lobby?"

"Sure." Mickie scooped up her shorts and disappeared into the building. I dropped back into the pool and began swimming laps with a long, steady stroke. I didn't mind losing the races. There are worse ways to spend an evening than with a pretty woman. All I wanted was a little company. Vivid memories of Dona were still fresh in my mind. I felt the stirrings of physical attraction toward Mickie. Her company would be a pleasant change. But it still didn't help resolve my problem of locating Sandoval. Maybe I'd come up with something later.

# Chapter Eleven

Mickie was sitting in the lobby. I wore casual slacks with a dress shirt and my only sports jacket. She was in a thin green cotton dress that stopped a good six inches above the knees. She'd curled her hair, putting a little wave on the locks. A touch of mascara on her lashes and a trace of lip gloss was all the makeup she wore. Or needed. I liked the way her dress contrasted with the gray in her eyes. A pair of black high heels brought her up to five foot five. I realized that when she was dressed up in her finery, Mickie appeared older.

"Hey, Reggie."

"Hi. You look great."

"Thought it was the least I could do, after whipping you so badly in the pool. You got a car?"

"Yeah, but I'm not very familiar with the area. How about you?"

Mickie smiled. "I'll drive, if that doesn't injure your manly pride."

"I'm all for equal rights. Where are we going?"

"Let's make it a surprise."

Mickie's car was a Mustang, bright silver with a red racing stripe. It looked like it was going forty when it was still sitting in the parking lot. She gunned the engine and roared down the ramp for the freeway, deftly zipping between two trucks. With the stereo blasting out the latest rap music, conversation was impossible.  I made sure my seat belt was fastened and settled back to enjoy the ride. Twenty minutes later Mickie pulled into a small restaurant that backed into the side of a mountain. The hostess led us to a table on the patio, where we could watch the sun slowly disappear behind the mountain peaks.

"You really going to stick me for lobster and a filet?" I asked.

Mickie's eyes couldn't hide the smile that her mouth was struggling with. "Going to welch on a bet?"

"Just hoping you wouldn't be cruel to my wallet."

She buried her face behind the menu and kept quiet until the waiter arrived. Then she let me off lightly, but not by much.  She ordered a gin and tonic, Caesar salad, and roasted salmon. I ordered salad, whiskey and grilled shrimp tacos.

"What brings you to Denver?"

"I'm writing a feature story on the baseball team. One of their rookies comes from my hometown, so they sent me out to do a human-interest number on him." Mickie paused for a sip of her drink. "You know, make the incoherent mumbling of a Neanderthal jock into something legible and interesting. Entertaining."

"You're a reporter?"

She set her glass down gently on the table. "Journalist. I've been trying to get up the nerve to go freelance, maybe sell some of my stuff to the national mags, but it's a big leap. Most newspapers are fading fast. Lack of advertising means they cut staff and sections. More people read online blogs. Or listen to podcasts. But as long as management back home continues to foot the bills and send me on location, I don't complain.  Traveling adds to the pleasure I get from writing a good story. And I love to drive! I like visiting different cities. Maybe someday one of these will break big. It's a dream to see my byline in the New York Times. Or reporting for one of the national networks."

"Where you from?"

"Fort Wayne, Indiana, home of cows, corn and not much for excitement. How about you, Reggie?" Mickie tilted her face down while trying to suppress her smile. "In town for the lifeguard competition?"

I enjoyed the banter and her wit. "Looking for an old friend. I'm on a little vacation and heard he was out here, but I don't know exactly where he is or how to find him. "

"What line of work are you in?"

"Military. Army. At least until a couple of months ago. I got the early retirement boot along with several thousand other soldiers." I sipped my whiskey, letting some of Jack Daniels finest linger on my tongue. Getting buzzed was appealing. But I couldn't let my guard down and risk making a mistake. Better to play it smart.

Mickie must have caught something in my answer, for she let the conversation drop. We were quiet through the salads. Small talk covered her driving habits and the easy way she'd beat me so easily in the pool. By the time the main course was served, we were content to watch the sun make its departure for the day. It was a comfortable silence. I considered it something more appropriate for people who have spent a lot of time together. Neither one of us seemed to mind. We got coffee after dinner.

"Tell me about this friend you're looking for," Mickie asked.

I shrugged. "Not much of a friend really. He's a doctor, a chemist by trade. His specialty has turned toward skin grafts. Supposed to be in town for some kind of convention." I shrugged again. "But I don't know where."

Mickie was thoughtful for a moment. "Maybe I can help you find him. Sounds like it's important to you."

"I really would like to see him. I've got news about a mutual acquaintance." This was no lie. I hoped to catch Sandoval before news of Duggan's death became public knowledge. Even if his body was found today, there might be no connection to him and Bookman's death for several days. And even with CNN and the internet, the news might never leave North Carolina.

"Have you tried the Chamber of Commerce?" Mickie asked.

"What could they do?"

She shook her head slowly and finished her coffee. "The Chamber of Commerce would know where every convention and conference in town is going on. You could also check the Convention Center. They could direct you to the site. Maybe even his hotel."

"You're a genius," I said with a grin.

She batted her lashes. "If only you were an editor."

Mickie drove a wandering route back toward the city, swinging the car up into the hills above Golden. We parked on a lookout spot, where we could see the lights from the city blinking as darkness fell. Mickie walked to the edge of the lot and climbed a winding footpath amidst the giant boulders. I followed. We sat on the edge with our feet hanging off into space. It was a long way down.

"I'll drive you to the Chamber of Commerce tomorrow morning," Mickie said quietly. "Convention Center too if need be."

"Appreciate the offer, but that's not necessary. I'm sure I can find it."

She shook her head and took my hand. "I think your story might be a lot more interesting than the one I'm out here for. There's a lot you're not telling me, Reggie."

"What makes you say that?"

"A hunch. When I go with my instincts, it pays off. I think you need my help. Or somebody's." Mickie leaned back to study my face. "How about it? Gonna let me help?"

Images of Dona McWilliams flooded my brain. I saw her driving me out to grandma's place, lying beside me in bed, changing her look in Hack's basement. And finally, with her throat cut open, courtesy of Bookman.

"I'm not exactly lucky to be around, Mickie. The last woman who tried to help didn't fare so well."

"I can take care of myself," she said defiantly.

With the sun gone, the evening air was chilly. I wrapped an arm across her shoulders and pulled her close. She made no attempt to move away. "Let me think about it."

She shrugged and huddled closer. "Okay. But don't take too long. It's getting cold out here."

***

Mickie came back to my room, fearing I'd slip out in the morning and leave her behind. She stopped long enough to grab some clothes for tomorrow and a digital recorder. I was cautious sharing details, fearing my story might end up on the front cover of some trashy newspaper next to a headline about alien body snatchers. Then any hope of ever getting back to a normal way of life would vanish.

"Tell me about this guy you're trying to find." Mickie was all business when she got settled in my room.

"Dr. Bartolo Sandoval. Ever heard of him?"

"Nope. Should I?"

"He's been around the block a few times. Taught at some college back east. Lately he's been working for a big corporation. Reznik International."

Mickie made certain the recorder was functioning and propped it on the table between the two full sized beds. I reached over and switched it off.

"Hey!" She swatted my hand, trying to recover the device.

I sat on the opposite bed, facing her. "You're right. There is a lot more going on. I'm willing to tell you the whole story, but only if we're off the record. At least for now. If word gets out to certain people, my life is over."

Mickie's eyes widened. "I knew it.  From the moment I spotted you working out, I knew there was a story here! C'mon, Reggie, give. Don't get all mysterious on me.  It's not like people are dying over this."

A rogue's gallery of faces danced through my mind. "Five have died so far. How many you want to know about?"

She gasped. "Five?"

"A doctor named Bailey died in an explosion.  A beautiful woman named Dona got her throat slit by Herbert Bookman, who then fell out a window from sixteen stories above the pavement.  I believe a young man named Cartwright died when one of his broken ribs punctured his heart. The most recent death was Wayne Duggan, a bona fide sewer rat. He had a heart attack during a brawl."

"Are you responsible for the deaths of all five people?"

"Indirectly. There are probably others I don't know about. And there may be more before it is over."

"You've got to tell me, Reggie."

I hesitated. "Only if it's off the record."

It was her turn to falter. "Forever?"

"Unless I can figure out a way to use the publicity to my advantage, which doesn't seem very likely, it's got to be off the record. This is a story you'll probably never be able to write."

Mickie squirmed across the bed until her back was against the wall, smoothing her dress down her legs. From this angle they were skinnier than I remembered. "Life's been kind of boring lately. I could use a little excitement. Better than a feature on a third baseman."

It took over an hour to tell it. I laid out everything from being hired by Bookman to my fight with Duggan Friday night. At the end, I dug out my army identification card from the inner lining of my duffel bag and handed it over. I hardly recognized the face on the photo anymore.

Mickie examined the picture. She even held it up to compare it with the real thing. "This is you? Vincent Tyrell?"

"What's left of me. Now you understand why it's so important for me to find Bartolo Sandoval."

She handed back my card and rolled off her bed, slowly pacing between the window and the door. The high heels were kicked off long ago. Mickie moved gracefully in her bare feet. "Actually, I'm a little fuzzy on that part. Why track this guy down?"

"Sandoval was the one performing the experiment at the lab prior to the explosion. He knows which chemicals were being used and the conditions. If anyone can trigger a reversal, he's the one. Maybe he can analyze my skin and learn why it keeps changing."

"That's a pretty big maybe, Reg ---- I mean, Vince." She was momentarily flustered and confused. But only for a moment. "Which name do you go by?"

"Let's stick with Reggie Dunbar. It's the one that matches all my current paperwork."

"But what if this Sandoval character can't do anything to turn you back to normal? Then what happens?"

I went to the window and stared out at the parking lot. "I don't know. Haven't made any plans yet. I've got to find him. Give it a chance."

"We'll start in the morning with the Chamber of Commerce," Mickie said quietly.

I turned to find her standing beside me. "You're still in? Knowing these guys killed Dona and tried their best to kill me?"

"They won't be looking for you out here. And they certainly don't know anything about me."

I studied her face. All I could read was determination. "You understand they will keep trying to kill me? To keep me from talking?"

"I'm in. Two people together can waltz right through whatever security they have." She slid her arms around my waist and gave me a quick hug. "There are ways I can help you."

"You're sure about that?"

We stood by the window for a few minutes without talking. Then Mickie got between me and the window and pushed me back toward one of the beds. The expression on my face must have been one of curiosity. Mickie just smiled and shook her head. When my legs connected with the mattress, she pushed me down onto my back.

"You're kind of tall for me, Reggie. But I like a challenge."

"Am I going to become a diary entry?"

"Maybe you're on my bucket list."

"Do I get to see that list?"

Mickie laughed softly as she climbed onto the bed beside me.  When we were face to face, the kissing started. It was surprising how quickly the intensity ratcheted up. I could feel the warmth of her body through the dress.

She rocked back onto her knees. My right hand was pressed against the small of her back. Without a word, I reached up and found the tab for the zipper. It flowed down so easily. Mickie gathered up the fabric and pulled the garment over her head. I took a moment to appreciate her demure, athletic body. There was no body fat on Mickie, which suited me just fine. I looked at her face. Her eyes burned into mine. What I saw was pure animal lust. With a flick of her wrists, she tossed her dress onto the other bed.

Still kneeling beside me, Mickie kept her eyes on mine. I had draped my jacket over a chair when we returned to the room. Now she undid the buttons on my shirt, taking her time, letting the anticipation build. She pulled me up just enough to get the shirt out of the way. Mickie dragged her nails down my chest before she unhooked my belt. She was taking charge of the moment. With her hands busy, she leaned down and pressed her lips to mine. Hard.

"Reggie," she whispered breathlessly, "let me show you some of the ways I can help you."

# Chapter Twelve

Mickie was the most athletic woman I'd ever been with. In the beginning, she treated sex like a competition. Mickie chose to be on top and moved as if we were racing. And she was determined to win. I lost track of the number of times she straddled me, one way or another.  In the end we were panting for breath, covered in sweat. Mickie collapsed on my chest. Just to prove I could do it, I rolled her onto her back and took her again, balancing all my weight on my knees and hands. Always knew all those pushups would come in handy someday.

Eventually exhaustion overtook us. We slept deeply. Mickie was a warm comfortable presence the rest of the night.

Morning came abruptly, sunlight filling the room.  Mickie preferred to shower privately. She turned on the national news when it was my turn and burst into the bathroom to find me covered with lather.

"You'd better see this!"

I turned off the water and wrapped a towel around my waist. CNN was on. The lead story was the discovery of Wayne Duggan's body. Neighbors called the police when his decomposing corpse got aromatic. Under normal circumstances this would not have been newsworthy of a national broadcast. But the recent publicity over the explosion at Reznik International and the bogus terrorist attack created a juicier angle. I groaned and sat on the edge of the bed as my face, complete with a physical description appeared on screen.

"Jesus Christ in a cardigan sweater," I muttered.

Mickie switched off the set. "What are you worried about?"

"They'll be alerted now. Sandoval and Reznik will be looking over their shoulders. I wouldn't be surprised if they tripled the security."

She gave me that brief glimmer of a smile and wiped some of the soap from my forehead. "They won't notice you. They'll be too busy looking for Vincent Tyrell."

"My picture just ran on national television!"

"No," Mickie said calmly. "Tyrell's picture was on the screen. You're Reggie Dunbar. You don't look anything like him. Except maybe the eyes."

She was right. I had forgotten about my altered appearance.

"Holy shit."

Mickie nodded. "Exactly. Your whole face has changed. All your features are different. Ever thought about contacts? Or maybe sunglasses?"

Reggie Dunbar didn't have Tyrell's coal black complexion, or his scruffy mustache and flattop haircut. Not to mention the scars from countless altercations. Maybe Vincent Tyrell died in the explosion after all.

"Go finish your shower. You're getting soap on the sheets." Mickie turned away, wiping her fingers onto the bedspread. "We want to be at the Chamber of Commerce as early as possible."

I did as she suggested. On the inside, I was still the same. But outside was an entirely different person.

***

# Fade Away

The Chamber of Commerce office made it easy. Of course, Mickie's press credentials didn't hurt either. She fed the lady at the desk a line of bull about wanting to interview some of the country's top dermatologists who would be attending the convention. The lady was more than happy to oblige. Ten minutes later we sauntered out to the parking lot, with a computerized printout of all the pertinent information for the conference, from the keynote speaker to the after-hour functions the society was sponsoring.

The meetings were being held in a hotel and conference center located in Lakewood, just outside of Denver. Mickie had reluctantly agreed to ride in my inconspicuous rental car, rather than her memorable Mustang.  She checked her makeup in the mirror as I parked beside the hotel. Mickie was dressed modestly in a beige linen suit with a silky ivory blouse.  The only jewelry she wore was a cheap watch with a big white face, which made the numbers easy to read. As I switched off the engine she reached behind the seat for a large shoulder bag.

"Know how to work a camera?"

"Just like a gun. Point it and shoot."

The look she gave me was anything but humorous. "Very cute, Reggie. Pay attention. School just went into session."

Mickie tugged two cameras from a smaller bag and gave me a quick lesson. The first was an older Ricoh with a fixed lens.  Good for distant shots. The second was a Nikon with a removable lens that extended almost a foot and could be focused to highlight the freckles on the subject's nose. There was another smaller lens tucked into the bag, along with a flash attachment and a box of memory cards

"I'm not expecting you to snap pictures of anybody, but if you know what this guy Sandoval looks like, you can make certain he's here. Use the Nikon to zoom in on him, just like binoculars. With one of those cameras around your neck, nobody will notice you. Chances are there will be more than a couple photographers and reporters here, covering the event for the different papers and medical journals."

I draped the Nikon's strap over my neck and returned the Ricoh to the camera bag. "What about you?"

She offered that shy smile. "I'm going to work on the scoop of the century. Wonder if they award Pulitzer Prizes to insubordinate reporters."

"That type always wins. Won't stop until they get the whole story."

Mickie winked at me. "Who knew you could be charming?"

"When the dust settles, you'll have one hell of a feature."

Mickie rummaged in her bag for a moment and came out with a blue laminated card on an alligator clip that read PRESS in large white type. On a small line beneath it were her name and a scrawled signature. She handed it to me and hooked a second one on the lapel of her jacket.

"Welcome to the world of journalism, Reggie. Ready to go?"

"Let's roll, baby."

We entered separately, not wanting anyone to place us together. Mickie breezed through the outer doors as if she'd been a frequent visitor to the conference center.  I wandered around, taking a few pictures of the exterior. The main conference was just beginning in the auditorium. I didn't want to dally for long.  There were four bored photographers along the back wall of the room. I joined them, sighting the Nikon on the back of any heads that even remotely resembled Sandoval.  Mickie finagled a seat up in the third row and was listening intently to the current speaker.

Over three hundred people were crowded into the conference room. Most of them were in their late forties or older, better than half of them male. That didn't narrow down my search any.  I stopped squinting through the lens for a minute and let the camera dangle from my neck. The conference room was first class. A thick plum colored carpet ran down the aisle between rows of padded chairs. Several prints of Picasso paintings held court over the proceedings on the south wall, each crowned by an individual spotlight.  Above the speaker's podium was a row of skylights that gave the room an airy, open look.

Too many people from the back looked like Sandoval. If I was going to spot him, it would have to be from the side or face to face.  I checked my watch. Ten fifteen. According to the schedule posted with the Chamber of Commerce, the next break would be at noon for a luncheon. I might have a better chance then.  Leaving Mickie inside, I drifted out to the lobby. There was a grouping of comfortable chairs and sofas on the Italian marble floor beyond the registration area.  I found a deep wing chair and dropped the camera bag beside it. The thick upholstery groaned as I settled in to wait.

If Sandoval was here, I needed a plan.  I couldn't very well walk up and say "Hi there, jackass. I'm the guy you left for dead back in Raleigh. Maybe you can stop my skin tone from fading away. I'd hate to be lily white."  That was not the engaging opening I needed for a private conversation in the middle of three hundred medical professionals.

I developed and rejected at least five different strategies for getting the man alone. There had to be a way. As a kid, I was never fond of improvising, making things up as I went along.  But all my time in the army changed that. Rangers are expected to adapt to any situation they encounter. Maybe I was thinking too much about it.

As I sat there growing restless, a black SUV raced up the driveway and screeched to a halt by the entrance. Two guys the size of linebackers burst from the rear doors and charged into the lobby. I swept the camera bag under my chair and snatched a magazine off the table by my feet. The two gorillas bounded to the reception desk, scaring the living hell out of the young female clerk.

"May I help you?" she asked timidly.

The one on the left was blonde with a stubble cut. He placed both palms on the counter and loomed across it. "We're with Reznik International. Where's Dr. Bartolo Sandoval?"

"He could be in the conference," the girl said, leaning away from him.

"What's his room number?" Blondie demanded.

"We're not allowed to divulge the guest's room numbers."

I buried my nose in the magazine, trying to disappear into the print. The high sides of the wing chair obscured my head from their view. I sensed Blondie's partner staring at me, but he made no move in my direction.

"Paulie, check the conference rooms," Blondie ordered.

" `Kay, Bert."

Blondie Bert reached across the counter and snagged the computer keyboard. Then he swiveled the monitor around and began punching in Sandoval's name.

"I'm calling security," the girl threatened, reaching for the phone.

"I don't give a hot shit if you call your fairy godmother," Bert grumbled. "Ha. Six thirteen. I knew he was here somewhere." He dumped the keyboard onto the counter and headed for the elevator.

I dropped the magazine in the chair and followed, swinging the camera bag over my shoulder. Blondie Bert was pacing in front of the elevator doors, cursing at the inanimate object to hurry up. I stopped beside him. When at last the door opened, he nearly knocked me over trying to jump inside it. I thumbed the button for the fifth floor and moved back toward the rear of the car. The Glock was in the bottom of the camera bag, hidden beneath the extra lens for the Nikon. Bert was a bundle of nervous energy, bouncing on the balls of his feet as the elevator began its ascent. I ignored his impatience. When the chime rang for the fifth floor, Bert moved aside just enough for me to pass. I turned the corner, waiting for the elevator doors to close. When the motor began to hum, I raced for the stairs.

He was halfway down the corridor when I peeked around the corner. Room six thirteen was at the end of the hall, closer to the stairs than the elevator. I watched him get within ten feet of me. Silently, I dug the Glock out and jacked a shell into the chamber. When Bert started pounding on Sandoval's door, I used the noise to cover my own movements of stepping in behind him. I jammed the muzzle of the gun against his neck and banged his head on the door.

"Don't breathe. I might think you're trying to get cute."

"What the . . ."

Blondie Bert tumbled from my grasp as the door opened and Dr. Bartolo Sandoval momentarily appeared before me. Then Bert's bulk rammed into him and both men tumbled to the floor. Before Bert could react, I stepped in close and clubbed him twice across the base of the skull. I dragged him the rest of the way into the room and slammed the door.

Sandoval was unresponsive. He must have banged his head on the floor when Blondie came crashing through.

Using the drapery cords for binding, I trussed Bert up like the blue-ribbon alligator he was and dumped him in the bathtub. It was tempting to hang the sign for maid service on his belt, but I decided against it.  Some people have no sense of humor.  Sandoval was slumped on the bed, his hands and feet bound together with the remnants from his bedding. He was dressed in a shirt and tie. A suitcoat hung from a hook by the door. His eyes were open as I squatted down before him. Sandoval's voice was not strong.

"Mr. Tyrell, I presume?"

"It ain't the ghost of Christmas Past. You expecting me?"

He inched his head toward the bath. "Security called earlier. We had no men available in the area. They insisted I remain in the hotel room until they arrived. This conference is of major importance. I am supposed to give a lecture this evening."

"Hope they got a backup, Doc.  Chances are you won't be around."

He swallowed hard and steadied his eyes on mine. "Are you going to assassinate me?"

"Rather see if you can cure me.  May be hard for you to believe, but I just want my face and body back."

Sandoval cowered. "I do not know if this is even possible. An attempt to replicate the conditions is not a guarantee of similar results."

"We'll talk about that later.  Now we'd better get out of here."

After untying his limbs, I yanked Sandoval to his feet and pointed him toward the door. He draped the suitcoat over his arm. Bert was still snoozing in the tub; a washcloth tucked in his mouth and held in place with a strip of a bath towel. I took Sandoval by the elbow and left the room, scooping up Mickie's camera bag as we went.  It wouldn't be long before Bert's counterpart Paulie came looking for him. Whatever moans and noises Bert might be able to make would be ignored by anyone in the halls or the room next door. They might assume he was having a playful romp to start his day. Few people ever get involved. Time to move.

I hustled Sandoval into the elevator.  We rode in silence to the second floor. Before releasing the car, I punched every floor button between us and the roof. If Paulie was hovering in the lobby, he'd have a long wait for the lift.  We went down the stairs quietly. Sandoval cooperated all the way. My nerves were tingling.

"You gonna try and make a run for it, Doc?"

He shook his head. "I am neither a physical nor a violent man. Knowing your background as I do, there is little hope for my survival. If you want me dead, it is beyond my abilities to prevent it."

I pulled him up short at the door leading to the lobby. "Don't write your obituary just yet, Sandoval.  You're probably the only one in the world who's got a shot at curing me. When that lab blew, it was your experiment that went up in flames."

"Dr. Bailey was pursuing…"

"Bullshit. I heard Bailey trying to shut it down. You wouldn't listen."

"It was an important procedure."

I grabbed his shoulders and gave him a shake. "How many people have to die because of that procedure?"

"Science is not without risks," he muttered weakly.

"Then you shouldn't be concerned about another trial."

Sandoval's face paled beneath his olive skin as his mind leapfrogged ahead. "I could not possibly recreate the conditions. The temperatures, the chemicals, the components . . . what you ask is impossible."

"Get real. You know old lizard lips Reznik would get down on his knees and kiss your ass in Times Square if he could have skin like this."

"But I cannot possibly control. . . "

"Don't be so negative, Doc. I despise killing. I really do. Cooperate with me and there's a chance we can all die of old age."

Sandoval thought it over briefly then nodded once. "I have nothing to lose by complying with your request."

"Your enthusiasm overwhelms me, Doc." I popped the door open and steered him toward the exit.

# Chapter Thirteen

Mickie was angry. She didn't like being left behind, a fact she repeated several times when she stormed into the motel room.

"I got you into that place. You'd still be running around without a clue if it hadn't been for me. And then you take off. . . "

"Sorry. Waiting wasn't an option."

". . . leaving me standing around like an idiot." She marched across the room and flopped on the extra bed, arms folded over her small chest.

"Being paged at the conference was a nice touch. Learning you'd bugged out really pissed me off. You should have seen the idiot driving the ride share to bring me back here. Acted like he was God's gift to women."

The bathroom door opened and Sandoval came out timidly. He smiled faintly at Mickie. "Hello."

"Hiya." She refused to give up her sulky mood.

Sandoval approached her. "Are you a prisoner as well?"

"Huh?"

"She's a friend, Doc. At least, she was until this afternoon. Bartolo Sandoval, this is Michelle Atwater. Also known as Mickie."

Sandoval pressed her hand. "A pleasure."

"No wonder I couldn't find him at the conference," Mickie muttered. "But how--- when--- what?"

"Dumb luck," I said.

"So, what's your next move? You've got the doctor. What are you going to do with him?"

Sandoval sat by the simulated wood table that served as a desk and turned on the early evening news. Obviously whatever Mickie and I had to discuss was of little interest to him.

"I need to get him to a laboratory of some kind. But I don't have any idea where to find that kind of setup. Chances are the security people from Reznik will be looking all over hell for him. They might try and keep it quiet. I expect the local cops will probably be involved before long."

Mickie peeled off her linen jacket and folded her arms behind her head. Sandoval hunched forward in his chair, channel surfing the tube in search of something interesting. I leaned against the wall.

"What kind of lab?" Mickie asked.

I had to step in front of the television to get Sandoval's attention. Mickie repeated her question.

"A basic laboratory will do. I will need a good quality microscope, a centrifuge, autoclave and some standard chemicals for comparison testing. Nothing out of the ordinary."

Mickie closed her eyes and fell back on the bed, her head against the pillows. Sandoval waved me out of the way and resumed his pursuit for the latest news.

"You trust him?" Mickie asked.

"Don't see how I can't. If he can recreate the chemical reaction that caused the accident in the first place, maybe he can develop an antidote. Or maybe I'm just pissing in the wind."

She blessed me with one of those bashful smiles and slid off the bed. "With your colorful use of words, you could have been a journalist. Maybe a sportscaster.  Give me a couple of hours and stay near the phone."

I caught her arm. "You got an idea, or are you skipping out?"

"I'm in this to the end." She stared directly into my eyes. "Hope to see my byline on the front page with this story someday. Trust me. I just need a little time to prowl. And I can do some serious thinking on my own."

***

Three hours passed before Mickie returned. Sandoval was asleep on the bed with his clothes on. I was digging chopsticks halfheartedly into a waxed container of sweet and sour pork. Food has had little appeal for me lately. My appetite was on a leave of absence. I didn't know if it was nerves or a side effect from the chemicals. Sandoval made up for my lack of consumption.  For a small man, he possessed an enormous hunger. Maybe being kidnapped made him hungry.  He polished off a quart of almond chicken, some fried rice, a bowl of wonton soup, and three egg rolls. That was topped off with a couple of fortune cookies.  The first fortune said, "You will live a long and prosperous life."  Number two told him, "Use your talents to help others." I told him he'd opened them in the wrong order.

Mickie swept into the room like a whirlwind her face flushed with excitement. She stopped by the silent television set, closed her eyes and inhaled deeply.

"Sweet and sour sauce and fried rice. Damn, Reggie, you better have saved some for me."

I handed her the carton and my chopsticks. She attacked it like a wild animal. "Didn't you eat today?"

For a moment she blushed with embarrassment while shoveling some rice off the sticks. "It's been a long time since breakfast. Looks like your buddy is quite comfortable."

I nodded toward his sleeping form. "He's out for the night."

Mickie started to giggle. "Yeah, he's definitely the high strung - nervous type. Got anything to drink?"

I handed her one of the two remaining beers I'd gotten from room service. She flashed a look of disgust while twisting off the cap.

"Coors?  You ordered Coors?"

"It's all they had. A beer's a beer."

"There are craft breweries here. You could have gotten something different. You're in Denver, for God's sake, not a desert island. They have IPAs and stouts. Not just Coors!"

I shrugged. "Next time, I'll let you choose the brews. Any luck with your research?"

Mickie refused to answer until after she'd eaten. She dropped the empty cartons in the garbage then flopped on a chair by the window.

"It took some doing, but I found a place. May not be up to the good doctor's standards, but it's got the basic equipment."

"Where?"

Mickie scrubbed her face with her palms and bit back a yawn. "University of Denver.  The campus is about ten miles from here."

My blank expression encouraged her to keep talking.

"Look, it's perfect.  Fewer students are enrolled during the summer. It took a little work, but I tracked down a graduate student who's teaching in the chemistry department.  He agreed to give me access as long as he can be there when Sandoval does the experiments."

I felt my brows knit together in concern. "What experiments?"

"The ones on you." Mickie stretched and crossed her ankles.

"A witness. What the fuck, Mickie!"

She shrugged. "Best I can do.  If we don't show, he's got no way of tracking us down. It's completely up to you."

I took the chair beside her. On the bed, Sandoval snored and rolled over. Despite the situation, he was getting his beauty rest.

"I would have preferred somewhere less public. And without any witnesses."

"Nothing else was available. I checked every source that came to mind. There are several private laboratories, but nobody's going to let Dr. Frankenstein come in and play. And if you start waving his name around town, those goons are gonna show up."

She was right. Somewhere out in the Colorado night, Blondie Bert and his buddy Paulie would be busy searching for our hostage. They'd have all the flights out of the airport under surveillance, as well as the train station.  Chances were slim I would be able to avoid them for long.

"Why does this guy want to be in on the experiments?"

"I'd say it's a combination of self-preservation and professional curiosity. I didn't go into much detail about your condition. Suggested that Sandoval wanted to do some fieldwork of a highly confidential matter.  It's all top secret. Sort of a priority one basis." Mickie yawned again. "Batted my lashes at him. The poor sap ate it up."

I considered it for a moment. Action in any form beat sitting around with my thumb up my nose, or some other orifice. "When?"

"Eight in the morning. There are no classes in the labs tomorrow, so we won't have any interference. But there's enough other activity in the building that we won't attract attention going inside."

I didn't respond right away. She had worked wonders. Finding Sandoval's conference was just the beginning. I didn't know Jack shit about metropolitan Denver. Yet Mickie had found a suitable laboratory for the scientist to attempt a few tests. I was impressed and told her so.

"Better get some sleep. We'll have to be up early to check the school out before going inside. I don't want to walk into a trap. Reznik's guys might have an idea what I'm planning."

Mickie stood up and stretched. "Want me to wake up Frankenstein there and tell him where his laboratory will be?"

"Nah. I need him well rested and sharp tomorrow."

"I'm going back to my room. Call me in the morning, half an hour before you want to leave."

"You're a very trusting person, Mickie."

She flipped one of the thin hotel pillows at me. "Not really. Under different circumstances, you might try something noble like sneaking out early to keep me out of the action. But I didn't tell you the contact's name, or where we're going to meet."

"Don't trust me?"

She gave me that playful smile that made her eyes dance. "Nope."

"I'm crushed. Especially after all the fun we had last night."

"You'll get over it, soldier. Besides, I'm not inclined to play with an audience. Call me in the morning."

I let her out, then locked and bolted the door behind her. Sandoval continued to snore. It was going to be a long night.

***

The morning roared in as ugly as any day in recent memory. The sky was filled with thunderheads, most of which were determined to deposit half a dozen inches of water in the city in the shortest time possible. There was no sunlight penetrating the cloud mass, no welcome winds from the west or south capable of moving that portable ocean to another area. We were drenched within seconds of leaving the hotel. Mickie drove my rental car. I kept a close eye on Sandoval. He was rumpled in yesterday's clothes and as sullen as the sky above us. Maybe he'd been expecting the cavalry to rescue him like something in a movie. Fat chance.

Mickie dodged most of the water hazards between the hotel and the university, keeping the car just under the speed limit. She did well, blending in with the morning commuters. The Glock was in my right hand, tucked comfortably in the pocket of the nylon jacket.

"Sure could use a cup of coffee," Mickie mumbled.

"Get us to the lab and I'll buy you a gallon of the world's finest."

She tried to smile but it didn't reach the corners of her mouth. Or her eyes. "You are such a sweet talker."

Sandoval slumped against the rear door and toyed with a button on his suitcoat. Yesterday I left it in the car. As soon as he climbed into the backseat, he shrugged it on. It was the first nervous gesture I'd seen from him in all the hours since he'd been kidnapped.

"Something wrong, Doc?"

He jerked forward, surprised to find my eyes on him. He moved his hand away with an effort and began tapping his fingers on the armrest.

"I am simply a little nervous."

I turned my attention back to the windshield. Earlier I had knocked the rearview mirror into an angle where I could see him in the backseat.

As soon as my head was turned, Sandoval began toying with the same button again.

"Stop the car, Mickie."

She pulled to the curb beside a bus stop and switched her emergency flashers on. I climbed out and yanked Sandoval from the rear. Several people were inside the shelter, waiting for the morning bus.

"Lose the coat, Doc."

The color drained from his face like a bathtub with the plug pulled. "What is the problem?"

I spun him around and peeled the jacket from his back. He struggled briefly in the rain. The lank hair was plastered to his skull. I went through the pockets quickly: wallet, hankie, room keycard.  Behind the second button I could feel a little wire moving up toward the collar, not more than three inches long. I was about to rip the button off when inspiration hit me.

"Get back in the car," I ordered.

He hesitated. Motivation came in the form of a quick jab to his gut. Sandoval fumbled his way into the backseat.  I faced the shelter and my eyes picked out a likely candidate. He was an older Hispanic guy, wearing at least two of everything.  Just inside the shelter's doorway, he watched the two strange men interacting in the rain. I moved toward him.

"Ever play the lottery?"

He shrugged. "Sure. But it is rigged. They are all rigged."

I pulled the cash from Sandoval's wallet and fanned it out like a poker hand. Six hundred-dollar bills began to absorb rainwater.

"Pick a number, my friend and win a prize."

The Hispanic guy flashed a grin of wobbly brown teeth. "Six is good."

"You must have a gift. Six is today's lucky number."

His hand closed around the bills, but I didn't release them. "There is a slight catch."

He shrugged again. "There is always."

I extended the coat by the collar. "Make sure this gets on the next bus. I would advise you against keeping it, for your own protection. It could prove to be very unlucky."

His eyes were the color of walnuts. They sparkled at me. "Perhaps the coat would like to transfer across town?"

"Perhaps it would. Any other useful items you find during its ride would also become yours." I released the cash. It vanished inside his palm.

"What if a person should ask where I found such a coat?"

I raised my palms. "It was in the bus shelter on Federal. Someone must have forgotten it."

He nodded and draped the coat over his arm. I trotted back to the car and Mickie drove off.

"What the hell was that all about?"

I switched the heater on and shook the excess water from my jacket. "You ask Sandoval?"

Mickie inclined her head toward the rear seat.  Bartolo Sandoval was still curled in a ball, holding his aching stomach. I didn't think I'd hit him that hard. "He's not talking."

"Our friend there had a transmitter of some kind in his coat, wired to the middle button. If he'd used it when I grabbed him, they would have found us. It was hot yesterday, so he wasn't wearing it.  Got left in the car last night. He put it on, even though it's still warm."

"You think he triggered it right away?" Mickie asked.

"Gotta assume he activated it when we started driving. Probably hoped they'd track him to wherever we go. We stop moving, they got a fix on our location. Rescue him and take me out."

"You gave his coat to that bum?"

"Mickie, dear, just because a man is down on his luck does not make him a bum. That gentleman was kind enough to help me. The coat will probably spend the rest of the day getting shuffled from one R.T.D. bus to the next. And if I'm right about that transmitter, those two jerks I saw yesterday will still be cruising around in circles by the time we get back to the motel."

"Pretty smooth, Reggie."

"Ain't as dumb as I look."

# Chapter Fourteen

We did a slow crawl around the parking area of the science building at the university. Nobody was watching. The few cars nearby looked like a typical student's ride. Mickie parked as close to the entrance as she could and we dashed inside. Sandoval was even more subdued.  We left puddles on our way to the chemistry lab, leaving squishy footprints in our wake. Mickie knocked firmly on the glass door. It opened immediately.

"Hey, Mickie."

"Hey yourself, Caden. These are my friends, Bart and Reggie."

"C'mon in."

We entered and I secured the door behind me. I didn't know exactly what Sandoval would need to do but didn't want any surprise visitors. Caden obviously was smitten with Mickie. He was chubby guy in his late twenties, with watery blue eyes and thinning black hair. A sparse mustache ran along his upper lip, dangling two inches lower on the right side than on the left. It gave the impression someone had gripped the left wing and yanked it off. The knees of his jeans were worn out. A thin flannel shirt peeked out from beneath his buttoned polyester lab coat. I shifted my focus to Sandoval.

"Let's get to it."

"Yes, yes, of course. We should begin with the bloodwork." He motioned toward a stool beside a laboratory table.

I took the seat and rolled up my sleeve.  Sandoval's hands shook. It took him three tries to draw a sample. Then he scurried over to a set of slides and a microscope. Mickie and Caden stayed out of his way, one table back, talking quietly. Sandoval fiddled with the dials, adjusting the power on the microscope. Then he studied it silently for a long minute. He straightened and shook his head.

"Take a look."

I put my eye to the scope. "What am I looking for?"

"Abnormalities. There are none. This could be the same blood specimen as my own. Or from anyone else."

Caden stepped forward, so I let him have a peek.  Satisfied, he offered a quick shrug and moved away.  Mickie took a look, then folded her arms and settled on the stool next to mine.

"So, what's next?" I asked.

Before Sandoval could respond, the door rattled as someone tried to force it open. The doctor started running toward the exit. "Thank you, Jesus! I was beginning to wonder—"

 The door exploded into a million fragments. I hit the floor, sweeping Mickie's stool out from under her in the process. She bounced on my back and dug her fingers into my neck. The laboratory table sheltered us, at least for the moment. There was a thud off to the right where Caden had been standing. Hopefully he was taking shelter.

Mickie was clinging to my back. I rolled her off, digging the Glock out of my pocket.  Getting to my knees, I watched Sandoval halt his departure and clutch at his throat. A shaft of wood, maybe two inches around, protruded beyond his hand. Blood trickled down the front of his shirt. Before I could stop him, he yanked the piece from his throat. A red river gushed up and out. Dr. Bartolo Sandoval tried vainly to press the wound together, but his life quickly flowed between his fingers.  He hadn't considered that removing the splinter would prove to be the biggest mistake he ever made. Sandoval flopped against the nearest lab table and died, taking my chances for an antidote with him.

Blondie Bert and his buddy Paulie charged through the remains of the door. They looked like a pair of stampeding elephants trying to avoid a battalion of mice.  Rather than alert me to their presence by kicking the door in, they must have taped a grenade to the frame and hoped the shrapnel would catch me. Without any concern about the consequences, they raced toward me at full speed.

The Glock roared with authority. Paulie, who was slightly ahead of Bert, caught the first two rounds in the forehead. He collapsed in a heap. Blondie Bert kept coming. I forced myself to take a breath and steadied my aim. He was moving fast, bringing up a large revolver to bear on my face. I wanted this one alive, at least for a few minutes. Minutely I shifted the Glock and squeezed the trigger twice. Bert's right shoulder turned crimson. The revolver arched over his head. But he kept coming. Bert was two steps away when he launched himself at me. We crashed into a lab station and bounced, sliding across the hard tile floor. His knee slammed into my groin. Bert's left hand closed around my throat.

"Gonna fucking kill you!"

Bright colored spots swam before my eyes. My breath was gone, sucked out with the painful intensity that crawled from between my legs. My lungs protested.

"You're dead meat, Boy!" Bert tightened his grip.

The Glock was still clutched in my hand, caught somewhere between us. All my efforts were concentrated on the trigger. If the Glock was wedged against my own guts, I'd be dead. But if I didn't stop Bert, I would die anyway. I squeezed. The pistol wasn't nearly as loud this time.

It was a long moment before there was any change. My vision was gone. Reality danced just beyond my senses. Was I dead? Was Bert? What about Mickie? And Caden?

"Breathe, Reggie! C'mon, damn it! Breathe!"

Mickie's voice reverberated in my ears. An enormous weight was dragged from my chest. My lungs inhaled sweet, wonderful air. I felt water on my face. Someone tugged on my arms, helping me into a sitting position. I blinked repeatedly until things began to take shape.

"Holy fuck, Reggie. You sure know how to keep a girl from being bored." Mickie continued to wipe my face with a damp towel.

"You okay, Mickie?"

"I'm a hell of a lot better than those other guys. Sandoval's gone. So is the first guy you shot."

She had me propped against the wall. Caden was bent over Bert, trying to stem the flow of blood from his wounds. It was a losing battle. With Mickie's help, I struggled to my feet. Bert was barely alive. The two rounds in his right shoulder had almost severed it from his body. The third bullet had entered from his left side. It was lodged somewhere in his chest, intimately close to his heart. I nudged his leg with my toe, mindful of the blood pooling around him. Bert's eyes locked on mine.

"Where's Reznik?"

## Fade Away

Blood bubbles appeared on his lips. "Should have squeezed harder."

I was still clinging to the Glock. I let it dangle just below his belt buckle. "Where's Reznik?"

"Go to hell." His chest stopped moving.

I slowly lowered the gun to my side. "After you."


***


The sun and the air were better here. There was no dingy brown smog that was almost a permanent fixture in the sky over Denver. Colorado Springs was just far enough away to put a comfortable distance between me and trouble, until things calmed down. Whenever that might be. I was lounging poolside, watching Mickie do her mermaid impersonation.

We managed to escape the chemistry lab yesterday before the police arrived. Mickie had the presence of mind to grab my blood sample from the microscope and syringe as we headed out. She had reluctantly gone through the pockets of Bert and Paulie and turned up almost four thousand dollars. We gave a grand to Caden, which was enough to ensure his cooperation. Since he didn't know our names or even why we had come to the lab, we felt reasonably safe leaving him behind. The rest of the money went into my war chest to finance our survival.

After running from the lab, I dumped the rental car at the airport. We took a cab back to the hotel. All our gear was piled into Mickie's silver Mustang. We headed south.

I had recalled the events leading up to the confrontation so many times that everything was blurring together. How had they found us?

Sandoval never had an opportunity to contact anyone. It's possible they issued him more than one tracking device. One should have been sufficient. I hadn't considered anything else. Maybe they implanted something under his skin. Or in his teeth. Or the heels of his shoes.

I will never know exactly how they did it. The only thing certain was that another bad guy was gone. It wouldn't help bring Dona McWilliams back, but in my mind, Bartolo Sandoval had an equal share of the responsibility for her death.

Three down and one to go.

I'm not giving up, Dona.

Earlier this morning, I noticed my arms were beginning to peel again. It made me wonder what shade I'll be this time.

"You're looking pensive. Which makes me nervous." Mickie wrapped a towel around her waist and collapsed on the lounge chair beside me. We were the only ones on the deck.

"Trying to figure out my next move. If I even have one."

She shrugged and used her fingers to comb the water from her hair. "You could give it up. Hit the road, become a vagabond."

"So much for any thoughts of a career after the military. I can't even collect my pension."

"Why not?"

"Mickie, if I show up anywhere and admit who I am, Reznik's goons will have me in a flash. With his power and money, no one will believe a word I say. He's bound to have connections across the country. Hell, probably around the globe. Whenever they catch me, they'll hang the deaths on me like a cheap necktie."

She nodded thoughtfully. "How many are we up to?"

I ticked them off on my fingers. "Bailey, Dona, Bookman, Cartwright, Duggan, Sandoval, Paulie and Bert bring the total up to eight."

"But you didn't kill Dona or Bailey. Paulie and Bert were trying to kill you. That's self-defense. Sandoval died because that chunk of wood impaled him. You didn't cause that door to implode. Paulie and Bert did that. What about the other three?"

I considered it for a moment. "You could make the argument for self-defense as well. Each of them was a threat to me, especially when they saw the way my skin changed. I've become the biggest laboratory rat in history. And the most dangerous. Sandoval would have preferred to cut me open and try to figure out what is bleaching me during an autopsy. They could have preserved samples of every organ. Then methodically do a comparative analysis. Skin cells, blood, hair. Like I said, a lab rat. The one to experiment on, not one doing the experiments."

Mickie unwrapped the towel, exposing the bottom of her swimsuit. My eyes tracked the movement and stared at her waist, hips and thighs. A lovely distraction. "Then Reznik is the last one left. I don't think there's any other way around it. You've got to confront him. Maybe you can convince him to call off the goons."

"Gotta find him first."

Mickie was silent. It took me a few minutes to realize she'd dozed off in the afternoon sun. My back was itching. I could use her help peeling off the dead skin. It was time for us to go our separate ways. Mickie had been damn lucky during the fight at the lab. The splinter that took out Sandoval could just as easily have punctured her lovely neck. It was simply a matter of bad luck and trouble. Or timing.

Who could say if the odds would favor her as well next time? I went back to our room on the second floor for a hot shower. It usually helps loosen the dead skin. Mickie was waiting when I stepped out.

"Reggie. I've got a plan."

That statement made me hesitate. She took my lack of a comment as an invitation to lay it out for me.

It was bold.

It was dangerous.

It scared the living hell out of me.

***

"No way! We've talked about this, Mickie!"

She stood before me, hands on her hips, a determined expression on her face. "We both know you saved my life back there. Let me do something to pay you back."

"You don't owe me anything."

"Yes, I do! Give me a chance, Reggie.  It will work." She stomped over to the window. Frustrated by my lack of enthusiasm, Mickie dropped into a chair. She wrapped her arms across her chest. "I don't see you coming up with shit."

Her plan scared me. Mickie thought she could track Douglas Reznik down by doing an in-depth story on him for the newspaper. She'd dig up his current activities then contact his known associates in the business world. With luck she could locate him for a personal interview. She might be able to pull it off. I didn't like it. Not only because it might not work. Reznik would have no reason to suspect any relationship between Mickie Atwater and me. What I didn't like was her idea of the lead story. She wanted to publish my exploits.

"It's too shaky, Mickie."

"Everything is shaky! Right now, the public will believe whatever shit CNN is spewing about you. Because it's the *only* information they can get. But when I write your side of the story, tell what really happened, it will swing public support completely around. The cops will stop searching for you. Maybe someone else will even step forward to help." Nervous energy had her rocking back and forth in the chair.

"Like who?"

"Who the fuck knows? Sandoval was just one doctor. There could be thousands out there with the ability and the equipment to find a cure for what happened to you."

I was sitting on the other bed, trying to pull the dead flesh from my shoulder blades. We were sharing a room. One guy traveling alone draws more attention than a couple would. And the next wave of Reznik's security crew would only be looking for me.

Mickie left her chair and started scrubbing the old skin off my back with a washcloth. Not being able to see her face while we argued was something in her favor. I couldn't tell how determined she was to carry on with her strategy. I still disagreed and told her so.

"Don't be an old woman, Reggie. This might bring Reznik out in the open. If I go public and make the attempts to reach him for his reaction or version of the story, you'll know where he is."

"I don't like it. They could try to use you to get to me. Putting you in danger was never part of the deal."

"Knew that before I signed on, remember?"

"Umm."

Mickie finished with my back and returned to the window. It offered a nice view of the pool and the mountains surrounding the hotel in the near distance. "Once my story goes public, what I know about the accident becomes common knowledge. I wouldn't be any more of a threat to Reznik than Dr. Phil. Or Dr. Oz. Or Dr. Seuss."

I pulled on a shirt and moved beside her. Every possible scenario I'd come up with hadn't amounted to a thing. Maybe a different tactic was the logical approach. What harm could there be in letting Mickie try her luck?

"How long will it take for you to write the story?"

Mickie's eyes were dancing when she faced me. "Six hours. I've been planning it in my head for two days. Give me a chance to knock out a rough draft and make sure I have all the facts straight."

"Do you really think this will get the public's support?"

She gave me a fierce hug. "Reggie, when I get done writing this, you'll be a bigger star than one of those action movie superheroes."

"That's what worries me."

# Chapter Fifteen

It took eight hours to get it perfect. During that time Mickie concentrated on either the phone or her computer. She'd been in touch with her editor back in Indiana, summarizing the story. The man was anxiously waiting for the copy. We went through the first draft together. Mickie smoothed out a few details. She kept to the facts and didn't gloss over the violence I'd faced. When it was done, Mickie emailed the whole story to her boss. I flipped on the television to catch the latest news while Mickie ordered dinner from room service.

The local anchor was trying to look serious and smile seductively at the same time. Despite this, he captured my attention with the lead story. The right side of the screen showed three small faces in a neat column.

*"Police investigators at the University of Denver have positively identified the victims from yesterday's shooting at the Olin Hall chemistry laboratory. They were Dr. Bartolo Sandoval, Bertram Willetts and Paul Provenza. All three were employees of Reznik International. Dr. Sandoval was a director of research. Willetts and Provenza were security personnel assigned to the doctor during his trip to Denver.*

*Authorities have no leads at the present. Some conspiracy theorists speculate there is a possible connection between these deaths and other recent problems at Reznik International.*

*Meanwhile, the investigation and search continue for the alleged terrorists involved in the bombing of a Reznik laboratory at the Raleigh, North Carolina facilities, including the leader, Vincent Tyrell.*

*Joan?"*

I switched it off before the female anchor could get a word out. I'd overstayed my welcome. The beauty of the mountains with their promise of peace and tranquility was rapidly diminishing. It was time to get the hell out of Colorado.

Fast.

***

The early morning sunshine nearly blinded me as the truck rolled along. An hour ago, I crossed the Nebraska state line and could feel the tension easing from my shoulders. The Rockies gradually grew smaller in my rear-view mirror. Mickie might be waking up soon, anxious to see the results of her story in print. Too bad I couldn't be there. I switched on the radio and reviewed the last twelve hours. The steady beat of the drums and wailing guitar chords from a seventies rock song accompanied me.

After dinner, Mickie wanted to stick close to the phone and computer. She was expecting a call from her boss. I went for a walk. In the lobby I checked the local paper online and found several used cars for sale. One caught my eye. A ten-year-old Chevy truck that a cadet at the Air Force Academy needed to sell in a hurry. There was still a bundle of cash in my pocket. Using a hotel phone, I made the call.

# Fade Away

The cadet, who was a kid of no more than twenty, met me at a bakery around the corner from the hotel. The truck was battered, painted black with a few dents on every fender. But the windshield was free of any cracks or chips and the engine purred like a lion cub. I checked it out quickly, from transmission to brakes, on a fast test drive. There was over eighty thousand miles on the odometer, but it ran well.

"How much?"

He winced. "The ad said three grand."

"Get real." I stroked a dent on the rear bumper. "This baby's taken a lot of lumps. I'll go two."

"No way. I need three in a hurry."

I was in no mood to barter, so I dug out my bankroll. "Twenty-three hundred, cash. Right here, right now."

His Adam's apple bobbed a happy dance. "Cash?"

"Mostly hundreds. Unless you want to wait until the bank opens in the morning. You got the title?"

He nodded and pulled an envelope out of the glove box. There was no loan out on the vehicle. He scribbled an illegible signature on the proper slot and handed it over. I counted out the cash on the hood, neat rows of crisp bills. He scooped it up quickly and tucked it into his jacket.

After dropping the cadet back at the academy, I topped off the tank and parked the truck close to the motel's rear entrance. Upstairs, Mickie was pacing the room. Her cellphone was in speaker mode, resting beside her computer. The editor had questions. Mickie was all business, but a smile kept playing across her lips. Her eyes were once again dancing. I watched from the doorway. Spotting me in the window's reflection, she put an extra wiggle on her hips. Then she jumped up, wrapping arms and legs around me. My arms held her close. We swayed together.

"Yes, David. Every fact has been verified by Mr. Tyrell. He's a wanted man. No pictures."

"What about a sketch?" David asked. "We could make his features a little blurry but still get the different shading you described."

Mickie unwound her limbs from me. I relaxed my grip until her feet touched the floor. She gave me a quizzical look. I bent to whisper in her ear. Mickie smothered a giggle, then nodded.

"I did convince him that an artist rendering will help convince the readers of the changes. You could insert the drawings in the body of the feature. There are examples of the shadings I've witnessed in the attachment."

There was a brief silence while the editor considered it.

"Might have a greater impact if it's in a sidebar. Then you can compare the different shades," David said.

I nuzzled Mickie's neck. She shivered, then pushed me away.

"Let me get back to you, David."

"Make it fast. This is incredible. And Mickie…"

"Yeah?"

"Great work."

She flashed a dazzling smile. "Thanks!" Mickie switched off the call. She tossed the phone on the bed.

"Sounds like he's interested," I said.

"It's going over the wires. Associated Press will pick it up and run the story. David's been in touch with the Washington Post and the New York

Times. They want it!" Mickie was so excited she couldn't stand still.

Despite my earlier reservations, I'd come to terms with the idea of going public. I sat on the edge of the bed. Mickie was caught up in the moment. She danced around the room, hips swaying seductively, eyes closed, clenched fists jabbing the air. After a few minutes, she bounced on the bed and looked at me.

"Holy fuck! This is the piece I've always dreamed about. My work is going national! This isn't some feature or fluff story. This is hard news."

"Glad it's working out for you, Mickie. But I'm still left in limbo, slowly fading away. And the cops will keep searching for me."

"Once this hits the wires, everything changes. I wouldn't be surprised if the feds started tracking down Reznik to ask him a few questions. David's already putting out feelers trying to locate him for any comments. He's received confirmation from Raleigh PD about previous issues at the Reznik International facilities."

No amount of debating could lessen her euphoria. I thought she might want to go celebrate at a saloon, but Mickie was waiting for her editor to call back. She didn't want to have that conversation in a noisy bar. Mickie wanted a different type of celebration.

Although my mind was a million miles away, Mickie knew how to get my body to respond. She eased me back on the bed and focused her attention on my lips.  As if by magic, our clothes disappeared.

Mickie took the lead. Her body pressed against mine, the soft silkiness of her skin igniting my passion. Each time I peeled, my skin was experiencing the sensual contact of a woman for the very first time. My nerve endings were on fire.

There was no conversation, unless you consider the grunts, groans and occasional gasps of breath as dialogue. At one point Mickie was gripping the headboard for support. Moments later, she moved lower, guiding me with an intensity that surprised both of us. Only after we were spent, bodies covered with the sheen of sweat, did she speak.

"You'll see, Reggie. You gotta trust me."

I did trust her.  It was everyone else that worried me.

***

We took a long hot shower together. A few times I cupped Mickie's ass and raised her to eye level for a kiss. The second time she wrapped her legs around me and held me close.  I didn't know if this was a reaction to the danger we'd shared, or the start of something else.

Mickie was in the bathroom drying her hair. I quickly gathered my gear. The truck wasn't directly beneath the window, but it was close enough. My duffel bag landed in the shrubs next to the building. I rolled the window shut just as she came out, barely wearing a hotel robe.

"Why did you get dressed?"

I shrugged and turned toward her. "Feeling restless. Think maybe I'll go for another walk."

Mickie blushed. "Didn't you get enough physical activity a few minutes ago? And a few minutes before that?"

"Walking is not physical activity. Waiting makes me nervous."

Before she could respond the phone rang. I eased toward the door as she grabbed it.

"Yes, David. -- I knew it was hot. -- I'd love to get an interview with Douglas Reznik-- Somebody must know where--"

The door shut softly behind me. The desk clerk gave me a couple of sheets of hotel stationery and an envelope. I scribbled a quick note to Mickie and told them to deliver it in an hour with a bottle of champagne.

Now as Nebraska unrolled before me, I thought about the note. Words were her skill, not mine. It had been simple.

*"Mickie,*

*For your own safety, it's better if you don't know where I am. If your idea works, then you'll know where to find Douglas Reznik. But if his goon squad is still trying to eliminate me, public sympathy be damned, they'll try to use you to get to me. It's better this way. Trust me.*

*Three rules. First, check in with your editor every afternoon at three, eastern daylight time. I'll contact him as Reggie Dunbar. Anything you learn, give it to David.*

*Second, don't try to find me. I plan to keep moving, with no general direction in mind. Reznik might have some people tail you, in hopes that you'll lead them to me. So don't try it.*

*Third, Indiana's close enough to Michigan to make this feasible. Contact a guy named Kozlowski in Detroit at this number. Koz will be expecting your call. He's an old army buddy who is with the Michigan State Police. He's big as a truck, meaner than hell and smarter than both of us combined. He'll stick with you until this is over, one way or the other. Don't worry about paying him. Koz owes me plenty.*

*Now drink the wine and nap out. The party's just getting started. No matter what happens, I'm proud to have known you. Thanks for everything.*

*Be safe."*

I stopped in Grand Island, Nebraska for breakfast and gas. There were several newspaper boxes outside the restaurant. I couldn't resist the urge to buy one. USA Today ran the story on page one, above the fold. *North Carolina Claims of Terrorism A Hoax by Michelle Atwater.*

I scanned the story, grateful to see the accuracy in the details. Mickie must be strutting about like a rooster. She was a gladiator, taking on the big guys. I hoped there would be another chance to see her when this was over.

My letter to Mickie had been the truth, with one exception. I had a hunch about where to find Reznik. Something clicked in my memory last night during my drive. A little detail I'd dug up during my own research on Reznik and the others. I was headed east, as far as the roads would take me. If the man with the moon-cratered face wanted to avoid interviews, he'd head for seclusion. If he wasn't there already.

My cash was running thin, but I didn't want to stop along the way and work. It was time to invite Kozlowski to join the game.  At the gas station, I'd bought another prepaid cellphone. There would be no known connection between us. Which meant there was no reason for anyone to be monitoring his phone. He answered on the third ring with a growl.

"How's the Polish Prince of Motown?" I asked.

Koz's voice was low and deep, complementing his size. "Better than you. Never realized you were such a publicity hound, Vin."

"What have you heard?"

"Read it and seen it. Local papers and the national news are running it as a lead. You gonna send me an autographed photo?"

I grinned. "Trade you for some walking around money."

There was no hesitation. "How much and where?"

"A grand would be nice. Western Union work?"

"Easy. Got a spot in mind?"

I gave him a listing in Grand Island. There was a Western Union decal on the window of the store across the street.

Koz verified the details. He paused for a beat. "Sounds like you could use a little support. I've got vacation time available. Still owe you for backing me up in Puerto Rico that night."

"Got a more urgent matter for you." I described the situation and my concern for Mickie's safety. There were no interruptions from his end.

"Don't suppose you've got anyone else you can reach out to?"

"I've already overextended myself. Prosser helped earlier, now you. That's all I've got."

Kozlowski chuckled in my ear. "Didn't know Pro was still alive. He's got to be the ugliest man I ever saw. Surprised no one's put him out of his misery yet."

"Guy must have a shitload of dumb luck."

"This gets done, head this way. You'd blend in fine in Motown."

"I'll keep that in mind. Send the money and look after Mickie. If you don't hear from her by tomorrow morning, call her editor." I gave him the number for Mickie's boss in Fort Wayne, along with her cellphone.

All humor left Koz's voice. "Don't worry about the girl. I got her."

"Thanks, Brother."

"Watch your six."

# Chapter Sixteen

Later in the afternoon, I was at a truck stop outside of Quad City, Iowa. From a booth in the rear of the restaurant, I made the call. A coarse male voice answered on the first ring.

"Crenshaw."

"Looking for Mickie Atwater."

A heavy exhalation of breath was audible on the line. "Who isn't?"

"She'll talk to me. Name's Dunbar. Reggie Dunbar."

"Mickie's not here Dunbar Reggie Dunbar. But she is expected. Try back in an hour."

"Tell her I called."

I broke the connection and headed back to the truck. My eyes felt like sandpaper and my nerves were taut. Another couple of hours on the road were more than I could handle. Exhaustion leads to stupid mistakes. There was no room in my life for errors. I found a motel thirty miles east and collapsed.

It was dark when I woke up. There was a steak and egg place on the other side of the parking lot. I wolfed down a T-bone with four fried eggs, hash browns and biscuits. All this floated on two pots of coffee. For half a minute I considered getting back on the road. Normal people don't drive through the night. I'd arouse less curiosity and suspicion by traveling mostly in the daylight. Leaving in the morning, I'd be close to Fort Wayne when it was time to check in with Mickie.  A detour wouldn't be a big problem if I needed to see her. Otherwise, I'd keep going. Reznik's hiding spot was a long way off. Good thing the military teaches patience. That is if you live long enough to use it.

The motel room was cheap but passable. There was pressed plastic furniture with a simulated wood veneer. A lumpy twin bed, a small television bolted to the wall, a dresser and a wooden chair with a bright purple cushion. I sat on the bed with my back against the wall, watching the national news. Mickie had been right about the reaction to her work. It was the lead story. A lanky brunette stood in front of the company logo, giving the latest developments.

*"Officials here in Raleigh have reopened the investigation into the mysterious fire at Reznik International. Citing information revealed to reporter Michelle Atwater, police and fire inspectors have returned to the scene and are questioning witnesses and employees.  The whereabouts of Vincent Tyrell, the man originally blamed for the explosion and the death of Dr. Oscar Bailey, remains unknown.*

*Tyrell, speaking through Ms. Atwater, claims innocence concerning the problems at the Reznik facility and the subsequent deaths of several people involved in the company, including Herbert Bookman, an executive with the firm, Dr. Bartolo Sandoval, a noted researcher, and Wayne Duggan, director of security.  Police officers from Raleigh and federal agents are anxious to meet with Mr. Tyrell.*

*Douglas Reznik, the reclusive billionaire, has declined to make any statement about Tyrell's claims.*

*Reporting from Raleigh, North Carolina, I'm Lisa Welch"*--

I switched the channel, looking for a decent movie or something to keep my mind occupied. Nothing held my interest for long, not even reruns of the mysteries which never failed me before. I was back on the run, trying to keep one step ahead of the bad guys. With the exposure from Mickie's reports, safety remained just beyond my reach.

I gave up and fell asleep.

***

Last night was the best sleep I'd had in weeks. Somewhere between one and two in the morning, I came to the realization that the outcome was entirely in my own hands. Now we would play the game by <u>my</u> rules.

I woke up with the roosters and ran five miles before the heat got too intense. That was followed with a hundred sit-ups and two hundred pushups. My muscles were still tingling two hours later when I crossed into Illinois. I flipped on the radio and caught myself tapping the wheel to the beat of classic rock songs that questioned authority and the pursuit of happiness. It was perfect mood music to prepare for battle. Physically I was ready for anything. Mentally, I fine-tuned my plan.

Even after my workout, it was before noon when I entered Indiana. I worked my way around Hammond until I found a strip mall consisting of a drug store, grocery outlet, a hardware store and gun shop. My supply of bullets for the Glock was getting dangerously low. I bought two boxes of shells and a cleaning kit. During my escapades, I'd lost the one Hack had thrown in with the gun. I debated getting rid of it, but finding a replacement would be difficult. A soldier can grow attached to his weapon.

I picked up some skin lotion in the drug store, along with a small first aid kit and a few paperback books. The grocery outlet had plenty of fresh fruit and soft drinks, which I loaded into the back of the truck. The hardware was more of a general store, with everything from yard equipment to toys for kids.  I bought two rolls of duct tape, one hundred feet of thick nylon rope, leather work gloves, a hammer, screwdrivers, pliers and a heavy-duty flashlight. I may not have been ready for anything, but I was certainly better prepared. Lunch was a platter of burritos and beans before getting back on the road.

The radio stations drifted in and out. Snatches of rock favorites echoed from the tinny speakers in the dash, mixed with an occasional pop or country song. I spun the dial whenever it happened. The music helped keep me distracted, allowing me not to think much beyond the task of driving. After a while, I noticed that most of the songs I'd been hearing revolved around people searching for someone or something. But whatever it was, it was always elusive. I wondered if there was a cosmic force on the programming desk today, playing selected tunes for that renegade on the run.  A more rational person would have turned the radio off. I was waiting for the newscasts, hoping for updates about Douglas Reznik.

If necessary, I could alter my course slightly to the south and cruise directly into Fort Wayne. But if Reznik's troops had mobilized and were hovering around Mickie, either in person or electronically, I wanted to keep some distance. So, I stuck to my original plan and called her from a rest area in Ohio at three o'clock. The same coarse voice answered.

"Crenshaw."

"Looking for Mickie Atwater."

A bored exhalation of breath, like a puff of smoke. "Who's this?"

"Reggie Dunbar."

There was a flicker of hesitation. "Hang on." The phone went silent and I checked my watch. I heard two clicks, then a female voice in my ear.

"This is Mickie Atwater."

"It's Reggie."

"What can I do for you, Reggie?"

The voice sounded odd. Formal. There was no warmth or any of the pleasant inflections that always rounded out her speech. There was only one way to find out.

"I just wanted to tell you how much I liked your article about the baseball player. It's nice to see young people from Fort Wayne doing so good." Referring to the feature she'd written before our excitement in Denver seemed safe.

The woman on the phone chuckled once. "Glad you enjoyed it. It was very special for me too."

"Gotta go, Mickie."

"Bye, Reggie."

Less than a minute passed when I broke the connection. It was hardly enough time for a trace to be run on a phone. Whoever I'd been talking to, it wasn't Mickie. We shared the same motel room, the same shower, the same bed. I knew the sound of her voice. I would have recognized the tone. But that wasn't her. The real Mickie Atwater would have managed a laugh and made some quick comment about my sneaking out of the hotel. Or she might have thanked me for the champagne. But this meant she wasn't available. Hopefully Kozlowski had pulled her out of town and safely into hiding.  Time to find out. He answered on the second ring.

"Yeah," Koz growled.  Maybe that was his standard greeting.

"What's up, Brother?"

That earned me a bark of laughter. "This girlie has an attitude. And a temper. You coulda warned me."

"Where's the fun in that?"

"Stand fast. She wants to shout at you."

There was a pause as he switched the phone to speaker mode. I looked around the rest area. Standing beside the truck gave me a chance to stretch. It also provided a view of all the vehicles here. No one looked toward me.

"You're such a fucking Neanderthal! Couldn't even say goodbye!" Mickie's voice filled my ear. The real Mickie. Not some imposter.

"Didn't want you to try and talk me out of leaving."

"Like I could have managed that," she snapped.

"You can be very…persuasive."

She laughed lightly. "Demanding. That's what you were about to say. Admit it."

"Same thing only different. Where you at?"

"Motown. This giant you sent wouldn't let me drive to Indiana. Was that part of your plan? For him to fly out to Denver and be my fucking bodyguard? Seriously?"

"I expected him to meet you back home. Not come to your rescue."

"Remember me?" Mickie snapped again. "Do I need rescuing?"

Kozlowski's voice took over the call. "Did a little digging into that Reznik operation. Too many people working security there don't follow procedures. Shoot first mentality. Best defense is a good offense."

"You quoting George Washington?"

"Him, Sun Tzu and Bill Belichick. Probably a few more.  Gotta admit it works. I didn't want to sit on my ass for two days while girlie here made the drive. Lot can happen on the highways."

Koz was right. I should have figured it out. Anyone could realize that Mickie had been in Colorado during the events at the university. Draw a line from there to her home in Ft. Wayne and it gives you an easy route to follow. Picking her up in Denver made perfect sense.

"Staying in touch with your editor?" I asked.

Mickie's voice returned. "Strictly by email. The giant pulled the battery from my phone when we met in Denver. And he won't give it back to me. Like someone would be tracking me!"

"Koz knows what he's doing.  Try not to beat him up too much."

"I'll do my best.  But what about my car? That's my baby. When am I going to get it back?" Her temper was showing. "And where the fuck are you, anyway?"

She had me grinning. "Running down a theory. Gotta keep moving. When this is over, we'll get your car. I promise. Meanwhile do what Koz tells you. Please."

"Since you asked so sweetly, I'll try. There's no pool at his house, but he promised to take me out on the lake. Friend of his has a speedboat."

"Sounds nice. I'll be in touch," I said.

Koz's deep voice echoed the sentiment. "Watch your six."

"Copy that."

I got back in the truck and continued east.

# Chapter Seventeen

Three days followed in rapid succession, driving, always east. I was making a pilgrimage, but not to any Holy Land. I was looking for the source of my problems. Knowing that Mickie was safe with Kozlowski gave me peace of mind. I had no doubt he would take good care of her. Hopefully she wouldn't drive him crazy.

Following Koz's lead, I pulled the battery from my phone. Each night I would plug it back in, just in case there were any missed calls or texts. No one else had this number. I liked it that way.

A string of cheap motels near Youngstown, Ohio, Waterbury, Connecticut and Ellsworth, Maine helped break up the monotony of driving. Each morning was a repeat of the routine I established in Iowa: a hard run, followed by a series of calisthenics. I was in training, getting ready for the fight of my life. The hardest part was before me. Waiting.

As time passed, Mickie's story receded from the front page and the opening segments of the television news. Occasionally there was a brief comment made by some law enforcement agency or other. No spokesperson came forward from Reznik International. The big man himself remained in hiding. Mickie had been hoping the publicity would force him out into the open. Reznik refused to make a statement about what really happened back in Raleigh. Unfortunately, his idea of dealing with the situation didn't coincide with Mickie's plan. He played it like a turtle, keeping inside his shell and away from the public eye.  Eventually everyone would forget about the explosion and the subsequent deaths. A new tragedy would take precedence in the headlines. Whatever sympathy there might have been for me would fade away.

My plan looked better every day.

While doing my research on Douglas Reznik and Bartolo Sandoval, I'd stumbled across a short piece in a society section about Reznik and the lengths he was willing to go to for privacy. It mentioned an estate in Maine, along the Atlantic Ocean. The property had been completely renovated to fit Reznik's personal tastes.  It was the ideal summertime hideout for a billionaire who wanted to avoid nosy reporters.

Not far from my modest motel room in Ellsworth was the scenic town of Bar Harbor. Quaint little shops lined the few streets, with seafood cafes, art galleries and boutiques.  Motels far classier than mine banked the road leading to the ocean. Fishing trawlers left the harbor each day to harvest the seas. High above the city, nestled back in the hills were the homes of the elite. Among them was the estate of Douglas Reznik. I cruised the area, searching for his sanctuary.

Following my morning fitness regiment, I familiarized myself with the territory. Reznik's place wasn't exactly in Bar Harbor, but in Manset, slightly south of the harbor and Acadia National Park.  The estate was at the end of the section fronting the ocean. Beyond his home the road twisted and disappeared into the village of Seawall.

I returned one evening at twilight for a better look at the property. There was a fieldstone wall surrounding the perimeter of the estate and a double wide gate with a security camera and telephone mounted on a cement pole.  The asphalt driveway twisted through the trees, making it difficult to catch more than a glimpse of the house. The dead giveaway was on the gate. The logo for Reznik International was emblazoned across the bars. A manicured lawn, the color of emeralds rolled lazily toward the house and the ocean beyond. I debated a frontal assault. There was no guarantee old crater-puss was here. If I was caught trespassing, the element of surprise would be lost. There had to be another way. I drove into Bar Harbor for a beer and some dinner, running attack scenarios around in my head.

After polishing off a gigantic lobster roll, I wandered the streets. My skin was due to begin peeling again. I was almost the color of coffee with a shot of cream.  Where would it end?

Would I eventually be translucent, with all my internal organs visible to the world? There could be employment possibilities I hadn't considered. I could visit schools when kids studied the human body, giving them a closer look. Or I could find a circus and become a sideshow freak.

But that was later. There was one name left on my list. One person responsible for my predicament.  The same person who would pay for the death of Dona McWilliams.  She had been much too good to die for someone like Reznik. Hell, she'd been too good to die for me.  Nothing would bring her back, but I'd get a sense of balance if I could make this last one, the most responsible one, pay for her life.

My evening stroll ended at the harbor. Most of the boats bobbing at the dock were commercial fishing rigs. I moseyed down the pier. The stench of dead fish and rotting seaweed hung in the air.  A glimmer of an idea began to poke its way through my mind. A fishing boat would be too big and cumbersome. Too memorable. I needed something fast and sleek. Maybe a rental. Or somebody with a side hustle. I headed back toward land, considering options.

Closer to the marina office was a branch of narrow docks filled with leisure crafts. The sun was almost gone and the few strands of lights on the dock would not be enough to guide me. I was about to give up and try again tomorrow when I saw the perfect craft. A fiberglass speedboat about twenty feet in length. Taped to the windshield was a For Sale sign with a phone number. I scribbled the number on the back of a dollar bill and headed for the motel.

In the quiet of the room, I powered up the burner phone. The guy who answered confirmed that it was his boat for sale. I described my needs, offering him serious cash to rent it. He agreed to meet me at the pier at seven in the morning. With a minor sense of accomplishment, I sacked out for a good night's sleep.

* * *

The boat owner turned out to be a guy in his early twenties named Sean. He had sun bleached hair in a ponytail that tickled his shoulders. Barefoot and wearing nothing but cutoffs, Sean's tan was so deep that he was darker than me. He was removing the nylon cockpit cover when I approached.

"You Reggie?" His voice was high and squeaky. Maybe his cutoffs were too tight.

"Yeah. You understand the deal?"

# Fade Away

Sean offered me a palms-up gesture. "Sounds easy. We cruise the shoreline so you can check out the scenic beauty of the area. If you see something appealing, we might anchor for a while so you can snap a few pictures. For this I earn a fast hundred bucks."

Sean believed the story that I was a photographer's assistant for an architectural magazine. "There's a chance I might want to return in the evening if we spot a promising location. You free?" I handed over a crisp fifty-dollar bill. It magically disappeared into the pocket of his cutoffs.

He flashed a row of pearly whites. "Do fish shit worm guts?"

"I'll take that as a yes. How many hours can you squeeze out of a tank of fuel?"

"Four, if we're just trolling. We can swing in and refuel and head back out. You're covering fuel too, right?"

"Yeah. You ready?"

"Undo that bow line and we'll head out."

Sean fired up the engine and eased the boat out of the slip. At first glance I figured him for a cocky, lead footed hot-rod type. But he was cautious as well as sure of himself. Sean eased the speedboat out of the harbor and gradually nudged the throttles up to a slow, cruising speed only after he cleared the channel markers. I took the passenger seat, which happened to be the one closer to the shoreline. Most of the homes were high on the hills. They had a view of the ocean but no easy access to the water. As we moved further down the coast, I wondered if I would be able to spot Reznik's estate. I glanced at my skipper. Maybe he would know which part of the shoreline tied into Reznik's place.

Sean donned a set of earbuds synched to his phone and was promptly lost to the music. Between the steady bounce of the boat on the waves and his swaying to the melodies assaulting his ears, Sean was transported into his own world. I returned my attention to the shoreline, trying to find suitable landmarks.

We motored down to Swan's Island, cutting a slow arc in the wake of the ferry boat that was returning to Bass Harbor. Sean hugged the shoreline, performing a drum solo on the boat's steering wheel to the music. I had to look past him to see the buildings on the coast. It took almost an hour for the trip down river. Going against the current, the boat bounced slightly higher in the waves. Sean found a steady speed that would decrease the pounding we were taking. We circled around at the mouth of Bar Harbor and headed back down.

Santa Claus must have been watching, because I got an early Christmas present. The wind had increased, blowing the flags with enough force to snap the nylon fibers. Most of the homes along the shore sported an American flag. Some included a Maine state flag as well. Twenty minutes down from the harbor, the man in the red suit sent me a message. High up on the shore was a trio of flagpoles evenly spaced across a large expanse of lawn. On the right was the Maine flag. The one in the center was the stars and stripes. But the left one was just for me. It was a large white banner with a swirling green logo and the letters R.I. in giant capitals. I'll never forget that emblem. Reznik International. Thank you, Santa Claus. I have always believed in you.

"Stop the boat." I lightly thumped Sean on the arm to get his attention.

He popped the earbuds out. "Find something?"

"Yeah. This is the place." I dug out the small camera from my canvas bag and snapped a few pictures.

"Want me to get closer?"

"Yeah. Close as possible."

Sean wheeled the boat around and brought me parallel to the beginning of the property within twenty feet of the shore. He cut the engine speed to simulate a trolling motor and we drifted downstream. I took about two dozen pictures, from a variety of angles. There wasn't much to tell from this level. The land by the flagpoles dropped off steeply to the ocean. A mixture of boulders and tree roots extended down to the water. Moss and seaweed covered every exposed surface. I could probably find enough solid material to climb my way up, but it would not be easy.

"What's so special about this place?" Sean asked.

"My editor's wants as much as I can get on the guy who owns it. Reznik's a hot topic right now. You know him?"

"Never heard of him. Does this mean we're done?" Sean shifted his feet nervously. It was obvious he had big plans for the cash.

"We still on for tonight?"

"Sure thing, Reggie."

"Let's go back in and refuel. Be at the dock by nine, Sean. I'll have some extra gear to bring aboard. If everything goes right, you'll earn a healthy bonus."

Sean grinned broadly. "Christmas in July, baby. Christmas in July."

# Chapter Eighteen

I treated Sean to a burger and fries after gassing up the boat. Then I left him at the marina and went to prepare for my invasion. A friendly lady at the library helped me load the disk from the camera into a computer. She even printed all the pictures for a nominal fee. At the drug store, I bought a pad of paper and several different colored pens. There was a dive shop near the marina that sold me a slightly worn wetsuit, mask and fins, along with a diver's knife complete with a sheath. They carried those surfing shoes with the rubber soles that were popular on the beaches. I added a pair to my supplies. I found a waterproof bag with a thick drawstring, a large magnifying glass and two medium length crowbars at the hardware. A pair of walkie talkies completed my purchases. It was time to prepare for my mission. I took everything back to the motel to get organized.

After examining the photos carefully, I devised two possible routes to get from the water up to the main lawn. Using some of the duct tape I'd bought in Indiana, I strapped the two crowbars together at their shafts, with the hooks flared out in opposite directions. For an extra advantage, I taped the hammer between the crowbars, giving me a three-fingered grappling hook. I fashioned a loop out of one end of the nylon rope and secured it to the handles. After testing the batteries, I stowed the two walkie-talkies in the waterproof bag along with the leather gloves. Every three feet of rope received a solid knot for gripping during the climb up from the water.  All the equipment was double checked and stored. It was as ready as I was going to get.  I stretched out for a nap, with the alarm on the phone for seven thirty.

* * *

Sean was on board when I arrived. He was sprawled on the bow of the speed boat, enjoying the last few moments of summer sun. He'd found a worn denim shirt with the sleeves cut off to compliment his shorts. I envied him. There had never been a time in my life when I had been as carefree as Sean appeared. He said nothing about the extra gear I dragged along but helped me stow everything where it would be easily accessible.

"What's going on, Reggie?"

"Been ordered to get as close to that place as possible. My boss wants me to get inside the grounds and gather as much information as I can. No access through the front gate. No visitors allowed, especially the media."

"You're gonna try your luck from the water?" He gave me an incredulous look.

"Get me close to the shore. I'll swim in and climb up.  Scout it out and see what I can learn."

"Done any rock climbing before?"

I nodded. "Been a while. But it's like riding a bicycle."

"That's no bike ride. Lot of sharp rocks beneath the surface along that wall. You fall, it ain't gonna be like skinning your knees in the driveway."

"Good to know," I said.

Sean rubbed his chin as though he were searching for stubble. "How long will it take you?"

"Hard to say. I might get what I need ten minutes after I reach land. Or it might take me several hours." I unzipped the waterproof bag and dug out one of the walkie-talkies. "After you drop me, go upriver a hundred yards beyond that property and anchor. Kill the engine and keep your earbuds out. I'll call you on this."

Sean turned the transceiver over in his hands. "You expect me to wait all night for you, Reggie?"

I pulled two hundred dollars from my pocket and slapped it on top of the walkie-talkie. "That ought to buy me four hours. Anything beyond it I'll double the fee."

The cash vanished into his pocket. "I suppose you want to use code names and stuff?"

"Sure. You're the Beach Bum. I'm the Midnight Crawler."

Sean shook his head in disgust. "Beach Bum?"

"Let's get rolling."

While Sean motored down the channel, I changed from the tank top and shorts I'd worn down to the dock into the wetsuit. A brief memory shot through my mind of when my own skin had been as dark as the rubber outfit. It hadn't been all that long ago. I shook it off and double-checked my equipment. The bag was looped over a belt around my waist for easy access. The Glock was deep in the bottom, wrapped in a couple layers of plastic. I draped the coil of rope over one shoulder and secured the crowbars and hammer. With the mask on my forehead and fins at my feet, I was ready to go.

Sean cut the throttle and eased the boat as close to the rocky shore as he dared. Ripping a hole in the fiberglass wouldn't do either one of us any good, especially since I was counting on him for my escape. Briefly I wondered how deep the ocean was at this point. I might have to make a running dive off Reznik's estate to avoid capture. Unfortunately, Sean's boat didn't have a depth finder. I 'd find out in one hell of a hurry if that became a reality.

Sean threw me a quick look over his shoulder. "This is your stop, Reggie." To my surprise, he extended his right fist. I bumped it.

"Like, later, dude."

With a flip, I rolled over the side and disappeared into the Atlantic.

The initial blast of cold is always a shock when you hit the water, no matter what time of year it is. I broke the surface, adjusted my mask and kicked my way toward shore. It was less than thirty feet between my drop point and the cluster of rocks that protected Reznik's estate. But the tide was stronger than I had anticipated. And it was pulling me downriver in a hurry. It took an effort to reach the last rocks on the edge of his property.

The boulder I grabbed was big enough for me to stand on. It jutted against the earthen wall that led to the main level. After shedding the mask and fins, I leaned against the wall, catching my breath and taking a moment to study the terrain closely for the first time. The wall was smooth and worn, offering little chance for leverage or support along the way up. The few rocks that did protrude from the rest of the surface were coated with green, slimy algae. This would not be a free climb to the top. Slipping on the new surf shoes, I uncoiled my rope and let the hardware dangle.

Swinging the rope in a slowly increasing arc, I launched my handmade grappling hook toward the top. The best guess was twenty-five feet from where I stood to the manicured lawn above me. My toss fell short and the hook came down quickly, clanking off the rocks.

I repeated the process five times. By the third toss I had the distance right, but the hooks didn't catch anything above me. I could only hope that Reznik didn't have this area under electronic surveillance. No one in their right mind would attempt to gain access to his estate from the ocean.

When the hook stuck, I had to force myself not to rush it. Repeated tugs on the line reassured me that the crowbars were holding, at least temporarily.

I tied the bag to the end of the nylon line and slipped on the leather gloves. Carefully, I began to climb up the wall. Even when I braced my feet against the earth, it was slow going. There was no way of knowing how securely the hook was dug into the ground. The image of my body crashing down to the rocks below was something I tried to ignore.  I concentrated on friendly faces. Dona, Mickie, Prosser and Kozlowski.

I couldn't let them down.

When my hand went over the edge, it was a return to reality. I'd made it undetected. After crawling over the lip, I scurried to the relative safety of the nearest tree. Slowly, I pulled the bag up from below and undid my grappling hook. Miraculously, it had wrapped around the base of the flagpole on the left. It was the same pole where the Reznik International logo flew. Karma. I dug out the walkie-talkie.

"Like wow, Beach Bum."

"Yo, Spiderman. What's shaking?" Sean apparently didn't approve of my own code name.

"My nerves for one. How you?"

"Lobster patrol is pretty dull so far."

"Hope it stays that way."

"Right on, Spidey. See ya."

"Out."

I tucked the unit back in the bag along with my grappling hook. After fashioning a loop out of the nylon line, I managed to work it over a limb about six feet off the ground on a tree just to the right of the flagpole. It was out of sight, but still accessible.

Keeping to the shadows, I approached the house.

# Chapter Nineteen

To think of Reznik's estate in Maine as a house was like calling the space shuttle a paper airplane. Reznik's place was a two-story brick building, with a tile roof and an open balcony running the length of the second story. It reminded me of a Spanish hacienda. I estimated it was over five thousand square feet of space. The ground floor was made up mostly of glass. Each of the four rooms I could see had multiple French doors on the outer wall, providing easy access to the occupants to stroll out into the moonlight. There was a formal dining room, complete with a massive wooden table and a dozen ladder-back chairs, a library where books lined the wall from floor to ceiling, a living room with leather furniture, a thick white rug and a fireplace, and a study which doubled as a game room. That included a billiard table, poker table and two antique pinball machines.

Time never works the same for two different people. Some never seem to have enough. Others are caught in the perpetual drag of daily chores. Tonight, time was on my side. Boredom must have been overtaking the four cretins on the security detail at the house. They had been ordered to stand ready for too long.

It had been more than a week since I'd tangoed in Denver with Blondie Bert. More than a week since Mickie's story was plastered across the front page of newspapers and network news programs and the shit had hit the fans. All that time and these guys had no action to show for it. They were floored, bored and ready to be stored. The four of them were lounging in the study, smoking cigars and playing poker while trying halfheartedly not to get stains on Reznik's designer furniture. I didn't recognize anyone.

It didn't matter.

I sat in the bushes outside the window, still wearing the wetsuit. The Glock was now strapped to my right thigh with one thin strip of duct tape. I wasn't planning on using it, but it felt reassuring resting there.

One member of the foursome was a short, stocky guy. He got tired with the poker game, (probably out of money) and headed out for a walk. He wore khaki shorts and a loud Hawaiian luau shirt which struggled to contain his gut. He didn't fit the physical standards of the usual Reznik security staff. I wondered how long he'd been on the payroll. Before he came through the French door of the house, I dropped back fifty feet and gave him some room.

Luau Shirt came out with a beer in his hand. Judging by the way he walked it wasn't his first of the night. He tipped the bottle back and finished it. Releasing a loud belch, he flipped the empty container in the general direction of the bushes I'd been sitting in only moments before. Luau Shirt headed right towards me. This was going to be easy.

He paused beside a tree and unzipped his fly. I debated between the Glock and the diving knife I'd picked up earlier and chose the latter. It was sharp, silent and shiny. Nobody argues with three S's. He was shaking the last drops from his joint when I stepped up behind him. One arm went around his throat, bending him backward. Luau Shirt went up on his tiptoes to maintain any contact with the ground. Both of his hands locked on my forearm, trying to break my hold. I flashed the blade before his eyes and brought it to rest against his dick.

"Jesus! No!" Luau Shirt was suddenly very alert.

I kept my voice low since my mouth was right next to his ear. "Tell me what I want to know, and you'll still enjoy the pleasure of a woman. Or a man, if that's your preference."

"Anything! Jesus Christ and the Holy Mother!  Don't cut me! I'll tell you anything!"

"Wise man. Where's Reznik?"

"Who?"

I flicked my wrist, increasing the pressure of the knife. "Don't be stupid. Douglas Reznik. Pizza face. Grand champion of the international butt-ugly competitions. Owner of this palatial estate."

Sweat rolled off him in layers. "Upstairs. Never knew his name. I'm just along for the ride. Pays five hundred a day. We're supposed to whack some Black guy for him."

"How long you been here?"

"Almost two weeks. Nothing's happening. I was gonna skip out in the morning. This place is getting to me."

"You and the three stooges imported together?"

"Me and Vinnie came up from Jersey. Nick and Ralph are West Coast muscles. Never met 'em before."

"Who else is here?"

"Ain't nobody else. I heard they're all out looking for the guy. This is the only place he feels safe."

I inched the knife a little lower. "Feeling safe, Jersey?"

"Fuck no!"

# Fade Away

"Say good night, Jersey." I shifted the blade out of the way and changed my grip on his throat. By increasing the pressure steadily, I applied the choke hold that knocked him out.

Luau Shirt collapsed in a heap. The duct tape worked well around his wrists and ankles. I stuffed part of his shirt into his mouth for a gag. I left him there with his weenie hanging out and went after the rest.

These guys were rank amateurs. I wondered how they'd ever been recruited. Rather than all three come out together, alertly searching for their partner, they sent one scrawny guy. He wore black socks in leather sandals, Bermuda shorts and a white oxford shirt. This guy couldn't decide whether to dress for the office or the beach. I hung back, putting distance between us and the house.

Mr. Indecisive headed across the lawn toward the driveway. During my earlier surveillance of the property, I checked out the vehicles lined up by the garage. There was a Mercedes, a Bentley and an Isuzu Trooper SUV. Made me wonder why Reznik didn't believe in buying American. It only took a few minutes to disable each one. Now I watched this second guy check the cars, testing the doors to make certain they were locked. He squatted down to adjust his hair in the mirror of the Volvo. He was very concerned about his appearance. I slipped behind the Isuzu without being seen.

Dropping to my stomach, I crawled beneath the SUV and waited. He had to go past me if he returned to the house. Ten seconds later he started back. Lashing out with my right hand, I caught his left ankle and yanked for all I was worth. He barely let out a yelp as he slammed into the asphalt. Squirming out from under the vehicle, I rolled to my knees with the Glock in my hand. There was no need to rush. This guy was out faster than the candles on a three-year-old's birthday cake. Blood trickled from his mouth and nose. Two of his upper teeth would need to be replaced. He'd live. I bound him with the duct tape and used one of his socks as a gag before dumping him in the trunk of the Volvo.

Two out of the way.

Two to go.

I heard a muffled noise and realized Sean was on the line. Digging the walkie-talkie out of my bag, I thumbed the button.

"Spiderman, Spiderman. You out there, web head?"

"I got you, Beach Bum. Somebody shaking your tree?"

"Absolutely, Spiderman. The water bear's been here twice already. Think I'll cruise once around the block. How's the party?"

"Kind of cool now, but I think the band's getting ready to play. Don't stray too far. You may have to pick up the gate crashers."

"For sure, web head. Always ready."

"Don't call me. I'll rattle your waves."

"Rock and roll, Spiderman."

I couldn't hold back the grin. He sounded like some of the guys I served with. "Rock and roll, dude."

Chances were that no matter how dumb these guys were, they would both come out looking for their playmates. An idea popped into my mind. Working fast, I might be able to get it ready. Trotting quickly, I headed back toward the ocean.

***

**Fade Away**

Reznik must be one nervous, desperate man to hire four incompetent thugs like these guys. Either that or he had such faith in the rest of his security force that Reznik believed no one knew about the Maine estate.

Old Pizza Face hadn't learned survival rule number one. Never underestimate your enemy. If he's still alive, he's deadly. If he's dead, he's no longer your enemy.

I had my trap ready. Rather than wait for the remaining two bodyguards to get curious, it was time to make my presence known.

Part of the decorative border around the garden was a row of slate slabs. I dug out a piece about the size of a dictionary and heaved it toward the windows of the library. Crude but effective. It made enough noise to get my point across in a hurry.

The remaining two guys charged out of the room. Several small floodlights came on, spread across the wide expanse of lawn. I hugged the trunk of a mighty oak and waited.

"Come out, come out, wherever you are." This original phrase was from the one on the right. He was the biggest of the group. Six-four and well beyond the two-forty mark on the scale. He wore jeans, sneakers and a golf shirt, which rippled over his muscles.  A small flashlight was gripped in his left hand, a large automatic pistol in his right. He held his arms crossed at the wrist, supporting his weapon with the other arm, as if it were too heavy to hold in one hand.

"You see anything?" The remaining guy was a string bean. He was six foot tall and one hundred twenty pounds on a skin-and-bone frame. This one wore cotton slacks, a sport shirt and leather boat shoes. He held a big revolver, probably a Magnum or a Ruger, in both hands and swept it slowly before him. My guess was that these were the west coast Boys. Mentally I named the bean pole Ralph, the one with the muscles Nick.

"There," Nick spoke softly, waving the flashlight toward the cliff.

"Looks like Joey." Ralph trotted ahead while Nick brought up the rear, scanning the area.

What Ralph the Bean Pole saw was the remnants of Jersey's luau shirt balled on the grass just beyond the circle of one of the yard's spotlights. He reached it first and bent down to retrieve it. Too late, Nick the Muscles realized what was happening.

"Get away from there, Nick!"

So much for my naming theory. Who can tell?

Nick the Bean Pole lifted the shirt, releasing the trip wire I'd rigged with a length of the nylon rope and the small limb of a tree. The limb had been pulled back as far as I dared and tied down with the line to a peg driven into the earth through the luau shirt. Nick released the pressure and things happened fast. Strapped to the branch was my homemade grappling hook. It caught him square in the chest as the branch came free, lifting him off the ground and sweeping him away like yesterday's litter. Nick squawked in disbelief and thumped to the earth against the center flagpole.

"Son of a bitch!" Ralph began to pivot slowly. When a bird flew out of a tree behind him, he swung around and fired off three shots.

I steadied the Glock and took careful aim. Only one shot was necessary. The floodlight behind him shattered. Ralph whirled and pumped two rounds into the fixture. Shifting, I placed one of my shots between his taking out another light. There were four staggered around the flagpoles. I knocked out three of them before Ralph realized what was happening. He used ten rounds from his clip before the gun jammed. I blasted the last bulb with a single shot. There was still a dozen left in the Glock's clip and one in the breech.

"Got no fight with you," I said quietly.

The wind had picked up. My voice carried easily to Ralph, but he pretended not to hear. Disgusted, he threw his pistol down and clenched his fists. I was close enough to see the knuckles whiten.

"You hurt my brother!"

"He's still alive. Take him and go. I'm not after you guys."

Ralph hesitated. I remembered the large revolver Nick had been holding when he'd activated my booby trap. The gun had gone tumbling over the cliff to the rocks below. Hopefully it was sleeping with the fishes. I moved away from the tree and closed the distance between us. The moon chose that moment to drop a few shafts of light down onto the barrel of the Glock. Ralph swallowed hard.

"Last chance, muscles. Grab your brother. Go in peace. I've no reason to kill you unless you try to stop me." I lowered the Glock. "It's your call."

Ralph almost made up his mind to accept my offer. Almost, that is, until his brother moaned in pain on the ground between us.

That was all it took to rekindle Ralph's anger. He bellowed a scream and charged faster than I thought possible. Before I could aim the Glock, he plowed into me, knocking the weapon away. It sailed over my head. Ralph brought his massive hands up to my throat and began to squeeze. Bright stars exploded before my eyes as everything started to go fuzzy.

Why does every guy I go up against want to choke the life out of me?

# Chapter Twenty

Ralph was a long way from rational. There was no strategy for his attack, simply anger driven to its boiling point. I coughed and gagged, trying to get my breath. That made him squeeze tighter. Slapping my hands together, I brought them up between his arms, trying to break his grip. It weakened, but Ralph was determined to hang on.

Desperately, I clapped my hands again with his head in between them. The pressure was enough to shatter his eardrums. He released me, staggering back. I stumbled dangerously close to edge, wheezing for breath. My vision began to clear.

"Fucking kill you!"

My eyes focused enough to see Ralph charging again. This time his hands clutched his aching head. He slammed a shoulder into me. We flew off the edge of the lawn toward the rocks below.

For the first time in weeks, Lady Luck winked at me. The nylon rope hung before me, still looped around the last tree branch. I grabbed it with both hands and swung out. Ralph's momentum carried him beyond me out into space, then toward the water below. He cleared the rock ledge and entered the ocean with the same splash as a killer whale, but nowhere near the grace. I swung back to the lawn and dropped onto the grass. After giving the rope a kiss of thanks, I hurried to my pack by the tree.

"Hey Beach Bum!"

"Spiderman! That you doing the swan dive?"

"Guy didn't like me dancing with his girl. Can you pick him up?"

"Sure thing. What the fuck do I do with him?"

"Run him to the base. Might need a doctor's visit."

"What about you?" Sean asked

"Looks like I get to leave by the front gate, Dude."

"What about my bonus?"

That got me grinning. "I'm good for it. Maybe the swan diver will kick in for the ride."

From the water I heard three quick taps on the horn. "Rock on, Spidey."

"Rock on, Beach Bum!"

Tucking the transceiver back into the bag, I moved over to give Nick a quick once over. He had managed to pull himself into a sitting position, his back pressed against the flagpole.

"Fucking bastard."

I ripped his shirt open. "Same to you. I'd be dead right now if you'd had the chance."

"Where's Ralph?"

"Went for a dip in the ocean. Friend of mine will get him to shore and some medical attention. He'll live."

Nick's body convulsed. Shock must be setting in. "What about me?"

I checked his wound quickly with the flashlight Ralph dropped. "Looks like you cracked a couple of ribs. Stay put and you'll be fine. If you move, you might puncture a lung. Behave yourself. I'll send an ambulance."

"I ain't going anywhere."

"Wise man."

There was little need for shadows now. I trotted across the lawn toward the house. The lights were still on in the poker room. One of the patio doors was open. I came through it fast. My faithful Glock was gone. It might have gone over the cliff or been knocked behind me into the shrubs. There was nothing to be gained by searching for it. The only weapon I had left was my knife. And the various types of hand-to-hand combat training from the army. If necessary, I could improvise a weapon. There was no way of knowing what kind of arsenal Reznik kept for himself.

At this stage I didn't care.

With every sense tingling in anticipation, I began to search the house. Each of the rooms on the first floor visible from the lawn was empty, as were the kitchen, laundry and storage areas lining the rear of the building. Cautiously, I moved up the curving staircase to the second floor.

On the landing I hesitated. Four doors ran the length of the corridor. For some reason I expected Reznik's quarters would be at the far end of the hall. The first door swung open to reveal an empty bathroom. The second was a guest bedroom big enough to sleep twelve. Maybe two dozen if they were intimate. The third was a lavishly appointed office, with a desk, computer and telephones. I stopped in front of the last door, wiping my sweaty palms on the legs of the wetsuit.

Reznik might be expecting me to come crashing in like Rambo, full of swagger and invincibility. In the movies, no bullet ever took out the hero. He was invincible. But this wasn't make-believe. This was reality. I left the door closed and cut through the office to the balcony. From outside I eased my head around the corner and peeked into Reznik's room.

The lamps were on. There was plenty of light to see by. A low murmur of voices carried through the window. A tall chest of drawers ran along one wall. A recliner was stationed by the window and a king-sized four poster bed in the center of the room. No mirrors. With a puss like his, I couldn't blame him.

On the bed was a feminine form with long blonde hair. I slipped through the door. Groans were coming from the mattress. She was bound spreadeagle. A mask covered her eyes. She was a big woman, large of hips, waist and boobs. A black lace teddy was plastered to her body. There was a thin sheen of perspiration coating her pale skin. I did a quick search to confirm we were alone.

"Who's there?" she asked shakily.

"Relax." I sat beside her and removed the mask. She blinked rapidly while I began trying to free her right wrist.

"He is one sick fucking bastard."

The rope around her limbs was knotted tightly. I had neither the time nor the patience. The knife slashed through the cords that held her in place. "Tell me about it."

She pulled the nylon rope from her wrists and began rubbing her raw flesh. "I'm supposed to get two grand for a night like this. The sick puke gives me half up front. Then he ties me up. We just got started when World War III kicked off in the front yard. The freak jumps off the bed and runs out, leaving me here! And he's not even halfway done with the nasty."

"How long ago?"

She shrugged then glanced at the digital clock radio on the dresser.

4:21 glared back in tiny red dots. Where the hell had the night gone? I realized the radio was on low, cranking out hits from the seventies.

"Ten, maybe fifteen minutes. Hard to tell, with the blindfold and all."

I noticed a thick wallet on the dresser next to a ring of keys. Flipping it open revealed several thousand dollars in large bills. I counted out a grand and dropped it on the bed beside her. "You hear anything else? Any idea where he was going?"

"Said the only safe place was the mountain. He must have meant Cadillac Mountain. It's in the National Park.  First place in the country to see the sunrise." She scooped up the cash and swung off the bed, tucking it into a leather purse on the floor.

"That's a hell of a walk from here."

"He took one of the scooters. I heard it going a few minutes before you got here. Sounded like none of the cars would start."

I watched her struggle with a denim skirt and a frilly blouse. "You said <u>one</u> of the scooters?"

"Yeah. There were two of them in the garage when I came in tonight. The jerk who drove me said these were the boss's latest toys."

On the radio a band began to sing the praises of round women.  I grabbed her face in both hands and planted a kiss on her forehead. "You just won the lottery." Giving her the rest of the cash, I threw the empty wallet onto the dresser.

"Thanks!"

I paused at the balcony door. "Drop a dime on the medics for me. There's a guy out by the flagpole who needs a doctor."

"For this much cash, I'll treat him myself!"

# Fade Away

***

In the garage I found the second scooter. It was a big Honda with a bright red paint job. The key dangled from the ignition. With a burp and a dull roar, I wobbled out the gate and started picking up speed. There was no traffic on the narrow street that led to State Road 102. I pressed it on the hills, leaning forward over the handlebars, cutting the wind resistance.

I must have looked like nightmare on wheels. Black surf shoes, a knee length wetsuit and my knife strapped to my left calf. Then put that image in a six-foot-two package and squeeze it onto a kid sized motorcycle. Not exactly a match made in heaven, or Madison Avenue.

I could not let Douglas Reznik get away. Not after everything that had happened in the last few weeks. If necessary, I'd drag this damned scooter up the side of Cadillac Mountain. The thought of being this close and going away empty handed would drive me crazy. It didn't matter what I looked like or my own safety.

I kept moving forward. Always forward.

For half an hour I pressed the little bike, sliding into curves barely visible in the meager headlight, shifting my weight as smoothly as possible. I had no idea how far the scooter would take me. Just about the time I was beginning to doubt my sanity, a dim red light appeared up ahead. It was small but steady, bobbing along the road at a pace that matched my own.

Reznik!

His light flared brightly for a moment, then swerved to the right and disappeared. I tried to mark the spot in the darkness in my memory and chugged on. A few minutes later, I saw the signs for Acadia National Park and State Road 233. Leaning right, I skidded through the gravel and bounced onto the black top. Up ahead, the red glow of Reznik's taillight greeted me.

We buzzed along for another ten minutes. I realized the night was beginning to pull back. It was getting easier to see him. Dawn would be breaking soon. I wondered if we'd see it together.

Reznik's bike wobbled and tottered then swerved to the right and dropped onto a side road. Nearing that spot, I could see the green reflective sign designating the national park and several hiking trails. Beneath me, the Honda stuttered and began to cough. So much for a race to the finish. I fumbled along the fuel tank, trying to find a valve for the reserve. It was still too dark to see clearly. I didn't want to risk crashing into a tree while leaning over to take a look. The engine stalled. I shifted into neutral, using the momentum to coast along.

When the scooter rolled to a stop, I dropped it at the side of the road and started jogging toward the park. All those recent miles of running were about to pay off. Ten minutes later I entered the park and turned toward the right, hoping this was where Reznik had gone. Up ahead was a small parking area and a trail leading to the summit of the mountain. The other red Honda scooter was lying on its side at the base of the sign.

My memory pulled up the rhythm from countless rock classics. All I needed was a driving beat to set the pace, to keep me going. It was time to finish this. Once and for all. I headed up the trail.

# Chapter Twenty-One

Going uphill didn't slow me down. I continued moving at a steady pace. It was that special time of day, with the sun beginning to rise above the ocean and the night slowly retreating behind me. On the trail ahead I could hear the crash of brush as Reznik stumbled along. In minutes we'd be at the summit. Time to end this fucking nightmare.

I crested the path and hesitated. Reznik was at the summit, probably looking for a boulder to hide behind. Or maybe a rock he could crawl under. If he was as ruthless about murder as he was about making money, Reznik would be standing there ready to fight. But that wasn't his nature. He could have faced me at the estate instead of running.  The advantage was mine.

Slowly I walked out onto the summit.

The sun was up, making its presence felt. Standing at the mouth of the path, I stretched my arms overhead.

"That's far enough!"

Reznik was on the right. He stood at the edge of the plateau, the sun at his back. Clutched in both hands was a revolver. He was wearing a pair of shorts and nothing else.  His feet were bare. His chest, arms and legs were covered with welts. Those could have come from the bugs he'd struck during his scooter ride. Or maybe that was his regular flesh. The rest of Reznik's skin was as white as a fish's belly. He was paler than any man I'd ever seen.

From where I stood, the gun looked like a small caliber pistol with a short barrel. I wondered if he was any good with it.

"Hell of a view from up here," I said calmly, taking a step toward him.

"Don't come any closer!" The gun wavered as if he were trying to center it on my chest.

"Amazing how peaceful it is. Might consider spending the summer here." I took two short steps.

Reznik's whole body was shaking. "Don't make me shoot you!"

"Give it up." Another step. "You're not cut out for dirty work."

"Far enough!"

"Your crew of trained assassins tried to take me out. All that high priced talent, just to silence me." I took two more steps, carefully watching my footing as I cut the space between us in half. Reznik managed to cock the hammer. The gun was shaking violently as he tried to aim it. Less than ten feet separated us. I wondered if he could pull the trigger.

"No closer!"

"Why did so many have to die?"

"You're a freak! We couldn't let you live. You were far more valuable if we could control you. Bartolo promised ---"

"Sandoval didn't know shit!" I stepped right at him. "He told me so in Denver. It would be impossible for him to recreate the conditions."

Reznik released the gun with his left hand and wiped the sweat out of his eyes. "The original plan was to capture you. Alive. Then Sandoval and his team would put you in a medically induced coma. Machines would keep your body alive. With the threat eliminated, Sandoval could test samples of your system. We could try variations. Mix the chemicals. Recreate the conditions. Use science. Understand exactly what happened. Learn."

"To find a cure? An antidote?"

"Skin like yours would be priceless. I would own the market!"

He sounded crazy. "The market?"

"Of course. Dermatology. Victims from fires or chemical attacks. People would be lining up to get treatment. Rejuvenated skin." Reznik was babbling now, the words blurring together. "No more scars. No blemishes. No age spots.  Gone! Every flaw. Gone!"

"Why kill Dr. McWilliams?"

Reznik waved his free hand wildly. "It was an accident. Thought you'd surrender. Why hurt the girl?"

"What about Bailey?  You blamed me for his death?"

He was still shaking, whether from anger or fear I couldn't tell. My gut said it was fear. "Best way to get police looking for you. No one expected things to go this far."

"It's down to me and you, Reznik." I was less than six feet away.

"You can't stop me! I have to kill you." His voice was shrill.

My eyes burned right through him. "Not fucking likely."

Both of his hands squeezed tighter on the gun. It was now or never. I slid to the left and dove forward as the gun went off.

There was a flash of pain, like getting burned with a hot wire. It was gone just as quickly. My hands clamped over his wrists. The revolver jerked toward the sky. With a grunt, I wretched it from his grip and flung it toward the base of the mountain. I looked down, expecting to see blood. There was a narrow groove above my right hip where the bullet had grazed the wetsuit. That was all.

Reznik stood before me, panting in exhaustion. He thought the shot had done serious damage. The confusion on his face was evident. "Who the fuck <u>ARE</u> you?"

The image of Dona's sweet face flashed across my mind. I grabbed him around the throat with both hands, hoisting him in the air. "I am Death, come a knockin'."

Reznik's eyes began to bulge. Struggling, he tore at my arms, cursing me to let him live. He kicked my shins with his bare feet. Moving another step forward placed him over the edge of mountain. It was a long way down. Finishing him would be easy. I could hold him out there for a minute. Then his weight would be too much for me. Gravity would take care of the rest. Reznik would be dead. As dead as Dona and all the others.

The realization hit me.

Reznik had always been dead. Inside that ugly body, he'd never been truly alive.  Reznik had never shared the comforts of another. The only physical interactions he could have were those he paid for, like the chubby blonde hooker back at the estate. His obsessions with power and money cost him his life long ago. I took a step back onto the firmer ground of the mountain and eased him down to earth. Releasing Reznik, I stepped to the side and gazed at the sunrise.

"You're not worth it."

Reznik dropped to his knees and sucked in deep gulps of air. I wondered if Dona would understand my reluctance to kill him. Too many people had already died. The price was high enough.

"I'll pay." His voice was a wheezing gasp beside me.

I ignored him.

# Fade Away

Clearing his throat, Reznik tried again. "I'll pay."

I started to walk away from him. It was time to get off the mountain.

"Money's no object. I'll make you rich. I'll pay."

The thought of accepting any amount of payment in exchange for Dona's life was too much. I whirled and threw my arms up in the air. "<u>Boo</u>!"

Reznik jumped backwards in surprise, over the edge of the mountain. He bounced several times then rolled like a beach ball all the way to the bottom, over fifteen hundred feet, before he came to rest against some rocks and trees a long way off.

# Chapter Twenty-Two

It was over.

I sat for a long time on the summit. No more people to chase, no more shadows to hide in. As the sun started heating up the day, my wetsuit became uncomfortable. Unzipping it helped but my back still itched. I didn't know if it was because of the suit or if my skin was peeling again.

It would be a long walk back to the motel. There were still a few loose ends that needed my attention. The bonus for Sean. A call to Kozlowski to let him know the trouble had ended. Talking with Mickie. Beyond that, I had no idea about how to spend the rest of the day. Let alone the rest of my life.

I headed down the trail, back to the parking lot. In a few hours the place would be crawling with visitors. Eventually someone was bound to find what was left of Douglas Reznik at the bottom of Cadillac Mountain.

There was no reason to hurry. I took my time going down the trail. Occasionally I heard snatches of music drifting up from below. I didn't know if it was real or if I was imagining it. A song with a great crashing of drums and cymbals echoed in my head. A fitting theme to Reznik's last moments on earth.

The path emptied into the parking area as a new song began. Mick and the boys promptly jumped in with an old favorite about someone you'd least expect to ask for a sympathetic reaction. Reznik's scooter remained on its side by the park sign. An old Ford pickup truck equipped with a camper was parked in the lot. The music was coming from the cab. The windows were down and the radio cranked up.  A beefy older man wearing worn jeans and a denim shirt sat on the rear bumper with a mug of coffee. A battered New England Patriots baseball cap was perched way back on his head. Neither my appearance nor my outfit seemed to bother him.

"A glorious morning," he called.

"That it is."

"Care for a cup of Joe?"

I closed my eyes and inhaled deeply. "If it tastes as good as it smells, you got a customer."

He chuckled once and reached into the open doorway of the camper. He brought out a ceramic mug and topped it off from a thermos that had been sitting by his feet. "Hate those damn Styrofoam things.  Make coffee taste like plastic."

"I hear you."

He handed over the mug. "How do you take it, Tyrell?"

I hesitated with the coffee just beneath my nose. "Name's Dunbar. Reggie Dunbar."

He nodded and sipped his own coffee. "Whatever you prefer. I'm Cedric True. Relax. Enjoy your Joe. I would never drug another man's coffee. Even I have standards and ethics. Well, some ethics."

I sat beside him and sipped. The coffee was freshly brewed, not instant. This guy was serious, whoever the hell he was.

"I have a proposal for you to consider, Mr. Tyrell."

"Dunbar," I persisted. "You a Belichick fan?"

He gave his head a slow shake. "Brady. The man is a legend."

"The best ever," I agreed.

"Gotta tell you, I really admire your determination. Am I to assume by your lone arrival this morning that Mr. Reznik will not be joining us?"

I shrugged. "You could say he took the express route down."

True dug in the pocket of his shirt for a moment and came out with a slim leather case. He handed it over and took a deep gulp of his coffee. I opened it and studied the picture and the identification card inside.

"Department of Defense, Scientific Research Division, Deputy Director Cedric True. Sounds pretty impressive, Mr. True."

"Call me Ric. 1 can assure you that the identification is legitimate."

True explained that the operation was part of DARPA, the Defense Advanced Research Projects Agency.  This was part of the D.O.D. DARPA had the best creative people in a variety of fields. Pundits would say they turned science fiction into science fact.

I finished my coffee and watched him refill both of our mugs. "What's on your mind, Ric?"

"Two points. Being with the scientific division, we have access to some of the brightest scientists and chemists in world."

I blew on the coffee. "Hurray for our side."

Cedric True flashed a brief grin. "Heard you are something of a smartass. I like that."

"Get on with it. It has been a very, long day."

"We've been observing you for some time now, ever since your appearance in Maine. You handle yourself well. Every step of the way. We can use a man with your talents."

"You offering me a job?"

True nodded slowly. "A specialist. With your training in the military and your obvious attention to detail, you could do well. And at the same time, we could have those bright people see about finding a cure for your… skin condition."

"What about the incidents with Reznik International?"

"All charges have been dropped. From what we witnessed this morning through drones with infrared cameras, you single handedly took out four guards at his estate. None of them have serious injuries. That is remarkable, considering their line of work. Amateurs should know better than to tangle with Spiderman and a Beach Bum."

Knowing that we'd been under surveillance during the night made me uncomfortable, yet I couldn't hold back a brief grin at the mention of Sean's code name. "What about Reznik?"

Cedric True finished his coffee before answering. "Obviously he lost his footing on the mountain. Unwise to climb up for the sunrise without the benefit of shoes."

"Works for me. How soon do you need an answer about this job?"

"Take all the time you need, Mr. Tyrell."

"It's Reggie—oh fuck it. Call me Vin."

True stuck out his hand. "Give you a ride back to your motel?"

"That would be a good start."

"We can go to Virginia tomorrow morning. Or the next day. That will allow you to resolve any unfinished business you have here. Give you a chance to see the operation."

I smothered a yawn as we climbed into the cab. "Tomorrow may be too soon. Like you said, I have unfinished business to take care of."

True put the truck in gear. "I am certain we can arrive at a timeframe suitable for both of us."

"Spoken like a true politician."

"Politics is essential to life, Vin."

"Thought that was music."

"I believe it applies to both. Gotta know that to play any game."

"I'll keep that in mind."

***

Cedric True delivered.  One day after meeting him, he handed over a thick envelope. Inside was a bundle of cash, two credit cards and plane tickets. He'd let me sleep for six hours.  Then a lengthy debriefing followed over a couple of steaks and all the fixings. My meager belongings from the motel and the Reznik estate were collected.  Sean got his bonus. It was well earned. True drove me to Bangor and dropped me at the airport.

"Two hikers found Douglas Reznik's body late yesterday.  One theory is that he climbed up the mountain to meditate and somehow lost his footing. Such an unfortunate situation," True said.

"Don't suppose those hikers happen to work for you. Maybe part of your surveillance team?"

"You have a suspicious mind, Vin."

"Damn straight."

Outside the terminal, he extended his hand. "Two weeks. You have all my contact information in that packet." We shook hands.

"See you then."

The flight was uneventful. It was a pleasant surprise to discover he'd sprung for first class seats. I appreciated the extra legroom. We landed at Detroit's Metropolitan Airport right on time. I grabbed my duffel from the overhead rack and walked into the terminal.

Passengers hurried past the gate, hoping to be the first ones to reach baggage claim. Kozlowski leaned against the far wall. Our eyes met. A smirk crossed his face as I approached. The big man reached down and squeezed Mickie's hand. She'd been studying the screen of her smartphone. Mickie glanced up, tucked the phone in the back pocket of her jeans and launched herself at me.

"You made it!" she gushed.

"Course he did. Man's too ugly to die," Koz said.

"Matter of opinion." My arms were full, holding Mickie. The bag was at my feet. "Owe you, Brother. Thanks for taking care of her."

Koz thumped me on the shoulder. "You know where to find me." He leaned in and kissed Mickie on the cheek. "Be good." He left us there.

"Are we really going to Denver?" she asked.

"Yep. That's where your car is."

"And we're driving back? Together?"

"Yep." I checked the monitors. Time to board the next flight.

"What are you going to do then?"

"I'll tell you all about it. Later."

# The End

# Mark Love

Mark Love lived for many years in the metropolitan Detroit area, where crime and corruption are always prevalent. A former freelance reporter, Love honed his writing skills covering features and hard news.

He is the multi-award-winning author of the Jamie Richmond mysteries (with *Inkspell Publishing*) ***Devious, Vanishing Act, Fleeing Beauty, Stealing Haven*** and ***Chasing Favors***. Love also writes the Jefferson Chene mystery series (with *The Wild Rose Press*) ***WHY 319?  Your Turn to Die*** and ***The Wayward Path***.

His independent stories include, **"Rules of Desperation"** and the novella **"Part-Time Criminal"** and the latest **"Fade Away"**.

Mark Love resides in west Michigan with his wife, Kim. He enjoys a variety of music, books, travel, cooking and exploring the great outdoors.

You can find him at the links below.

https://motownmysteries.com
http://www.amazon.com/-/e/B009P7HVZQ
https://www.facebook.com/MarkLoveAuthor
https://www.instagram.com/motownmysteries
https://www.threads.net/@motownmysteries